DEATH'S CAPTIVE

Will she escape eternal confinement?

Scarlett Reed

Death's Captive by Scarlett Reed
Published by Crimson Quills

Copyright © 2019 by Scarlett Reed

Ebook ISBN: 978-0-6487293-0-3

Follow me on:

Instragram: @authorscarlettreed

Facebook: Scarlett Reed

authorscarlettreed@gmail.com

Book cover by:Jae Smith: Instagram @thelittle-fox96

Author photo: Olya Hilton from OH Photos

Acknowledgements:

Thanks to everyone who helped make this book possible: my mum Pauline, an experienced document editor, for helping with the tedious editing process whilst educating me in grammar and spelling and how to improve my writing style; my aunty Sandra, for being my proof-reader and picking up on the errors that we missed; graphic designer, Jae Smith, who even with a damaged wrist still designed a beautiful book cover that encompasses the symbology of my work; photographer Olya Hilton, for my author's picture that truly resonates with my love of everything pinup. Thank you also to my beta readers who gave me wonderful feedback and critically analysed my work before I released it to the public. I truly hope that if you've enjoyed my story you'll leave a review and follow me on Instagram for the latest updates on my future releases.

CHAPTER 1

I f a bird must live in a cage at least it should be a gilded one with fresh sprigs woven through the golden bars to make it feel homely. Maybe that's why I've always liked this hospital – it's modern and new. It can be daunting, and sometimes I feel out of place, but it's a pretty cage to be trapped in. The hospital grounds are pleasant to wander through, and although the corridors are flooded in harsh florescent lighting, they're clean and wide.

When I'm not busy I follow the nurses around the wards. I try to follow a different nurse each time, though I admit, I do have favourites. I pretend I'm one of them; going about my everyday life, looking forward to seeing friends on my days off, thinking about what to have for dinner, wondering how my family is, or worrying about the future. I haven't had those kinds of thoughts in years and it's nice to pretend.

Ooh the old blonde one is on the move. Margie her name is. I always wonder where she's going. She has a thick skin and a steel stomach. I like that. I wish I was like her. I think I was too sensitive and squeamish, which, during an emergency, isn't desirable in a nurse.

I follow behind Margie casually - she isn't moving with any great speed. She looks troubled; perhaps she's thinking about her husband. I've heard her telling the other nurses about how her husband drinks when she's not home. It worries her. I remember when Margie and Peter started going steady. She was so happy. Always smiling and humming to herself as she did her rounds. I remember when they fell in love and got married. Such a long time ago now – must be thirty years by now. Margie looks sad. I don't know why and it bothers me a bit.

Margie is coming to the end of the hall where a police officer is leaning against a wall, pencil poised over a folded newspaper. He sees Margie and swiftly puts it away. He opens the door for her with a smile and a nod. It's a fake smile. How do I know it's a fake smile? It doesn't reach his eyes. He's just acknowledging she's there, late at night, like him. I follow Margie into the room. It's dark. She walks straight over to the bed and turns on a lamp.

The male patient is asleep, but the brightness of the light wakes him and the handcuffs on his wrist clinks against the metal bed railing. Someone else is in the room, hunched over in the corner, perhaps asleep. He's wearing similar clothes to the man at the outside the room. Another police officer? Margie tells the patient she needs to collect some blood for testing. The man grunts in reply but doesn't move. Margie lifts the old man's arm and clicks the tourniquet in place, pulling it tight and pinching his skin painfully. He glares at Margie, with fury in his eyes. Margie smiles. She smiles? I've never seen her be sadistic before. She can be rude at times, particularly when the patient is abrupt and sarcastic, but never cruel. This behaviour is out of character. I wonder what's going on – I can get so confused sometimes; if I don't pay attention time slips away from me like I'm a goldfish in a bowl. Margie finds a vein and plunges the needle in, dragging the blood out into the syringe. The man winces and takes a deep breath.

"Finished," Margie says smiling.

"Is that the best you can do?" the man says, his narrowed eyes glaring into hers.

Margie looms close to the elderly man's ear and whispers, "That's a speck on what you deserve, you innocence-thieving prick." Margie straightens up, collects her equipment and leaves the room; I follow her.

Outside the room, the officer doesn't look up from his crossword puzzle. Margie walks off into a side room and picks a purple and a yellow topped tube. Stabbing the seals with the needle, she deposits the blood from the syringe into the vials. I watch as she labels the tubes of blood and sets them aside for processing. I wait in the doorway as Margie stares at the blood, seemingly mesmerised. Gathering herself, she places the vials in the rack beside the centrifuge. Margie moves briskly to the door, then hesitates, holding her hand on the doorknob. Her brow furrows as she takes a slow, deep breath. She turns her head towards the rack, and locks the door with a quiet click.

I roll my eyes at the irony of this action. She closed the door for privacy, but nothing is private while I'm around. I walk through the door into the room and lean against the wall. I haven't missed anything. Margie is standing beside the counter, looking down at the vial of blood lightly held in her hand. I am brimming with curiosity – seconds seem to tick by like hours then Margie opens her hand and watches the vials roll off her fingertips and onto the floor. She collects them up and raises her hands high above her head then drops them again and again with more force with each drop. I'm really confused because her face looks angry and determined, but I can see there are tears glistening in her eyes. She picks up the tubes once more and throws them with such velocity that I'm sure the plastic must crack and there'll be blood spilling onto the floor, but it doesn't. Strangely, Margie seems satisfied with her work as she places the blood back on the rack to be processed by the lab. She wipes her hands across her eyes, takes a deep breath, unlocks the door and marches down the corridor towards the nurses' station.

TING!

I'm so shocked by Margie's behaviour that I almost let her get out of my sight before I rush down the corridor behind her. I'm desperate to know what's going on but unsure how I'll find out unless she confides in someone while I'm within earshot.

TING!

We approach the nurses' station together. "Everything OK, Marg?" asks a young nurse, whose pretty face isn't spoiled by her chestnut hair being pulled back into a tight ponytail.

TING!

Oh go away! I think to myself.

"Yeah, it's just the patient in room 736" Margie replies.

TING! TING!

"The one with the guards? Isn't he..."

The world begins to ripple and distort. Christ! Not again. I never get to know what's what.

I find myself in the geriatric ward in front of a bed. I sigh. Duty calls.

CHAPTER 2

An elderly man lies in front of me. He is alone; a withered husk of the man he once was. I always feel sad when I see what the ravages of time do the human body, it doesn't seem fair. I walk to the side of his bed and sit. His breathing is laboured and his eyes are a milky haze. It's funny how it's only on the brink of death that people can see me. He seems to sense my presence first, and then turns towards me as I sit on the edge of his bed. His voice is a rasping crackle, "I'm not ready".

"I know." It's all I can think to say. I can feel his body is tired, but his soul is clinging on.

"Then why?" he asks.

"Because it's time to let go".

This fragile man is so dehydrated he can hardly muster a single tear. I look to the bedside table and see an old picture of a couple on their wedding day. It's hard to believe the groom is the shrivelled man who is before me.

"Where is your wife?" I ask.

"Gone." He replies.

"I'm sorry."

"Our daughter will bring her back in the morning to see me."

"Oh," is all I can muster in reply. I am caught for a moment, embarrassed. Usually in these situations 'gone' means dead.

The man continues, "Please, let me say goodbye to them." He reaches out to touch me. I stand, avoiding his touch, and say: "I can't, it doesn't work like that."

The man doesn't argue; he seems oddly accepting of his fate.

"What's on the other side?" he asks.

"I don't know; I've never been. I'm just here to help you get there."

I sit back on the edge of the bed and place my hand over his, temporarily pushing through the veil that separates our worlds to feel the paper thin texture of his skin. I've always hated this part. It doesn't feel right. I think about what the person is leaving behind; whether their life mattered. What they would have done differently. I listen as the man draws his final crackling breath. The machine monitoring his vital signs begins to bleep and whine. I pull the old man out of his body and clutch him to my side as a plump middle-aged nurse enters the room, followed by a bleary-eyed young doctor.

"Am I really dead?" The man looks down at his old frail body as the doctor and nurse swarm over his lifeless form.

"Yes." I reply. "Do you want to see this?" I gesture towards the medical staff trying to resuscitate the elderly man.

"Why would I want to see this?" the man gapes.

"I don't know. I guess it gives some people closure."

I begin to walk out of the room and into the corridor, and gesture towards the man to follow me, except he's not old anymore; he looks barely seventeen.

An orderly pushing an empty wheelchair walks straight through us, shocking the newly-dead man. He pats his hands over his body to ensure he is intact.

"What now?" he asks.

"I don't know," I reply in earnest. "Every death is different."

"Michael?" We turn towards the voice and there stands a barefoot girl with blonde hair, wearing a cream dress.

The girl sees the man's young face and smiles at him. "Michael, let's go," she blushes and looks at the floor.

"Mary?" the man says, "Where are we going?"

"Down to the river at the back of my house, silly. We always go there after class. Remember?" The girl's spirit looks almost confused.

The man brushes back his short blonde hair and walks over to the barefoot girl. I notice he is also barefoot, wearing faded blue shorts and a white shirt. He doesn't look back at me, only forward as he grabs Mary's hand and they walk into a bright warm light through which they can see beyond, but I cannot.

I like to think they go back to that river behind her house, but I think it's different for every person. I wish I knew what was beyond.

"Mary slipped on a mossy rock, fell unconscious into the water and drowned. Dying at the tender age of fifteen. Isn't life just heartbreakingly cruel sometimes?" There's a sneer in his voice followed by a snide chuckle.

"How nice of you to pop in at this tender moment, Niklaus." My voice is brimming with sarcasm as I address the tall, dark-haired man standing by my side. I look up into his face, which seems cool and sculpted like a marble statue.

Niklaus looks towards me with an intensity that is hard to interpret: "You never love anyone like your first. Some people spend the rest of their life trying to recreate it. Such a shame that only in death one can acquire it."

"Why are you so cynical? That man, Michael, is happy with his wife. They had a family together. He asked me if he could stay just a little longer so he could say goodbye to them..."

Niklaus raises his hand to cut off my sentence. I stand silent. His face comes close to mine. "Everybody always asks to stay a little longer – there are few exceptions."

I look back down the corridor where the bright light was. It is true what he said. I can feel Niklaus move behind me and put his hands on my shoulders. I try not to stiffen. I can hear him breathing as he says gently in my ear, "Besides the real question you've got to ask yourself is how happy was Michael with his wife? You saw just as I did, Michael walking off into a beautiful portal of light with another woman."

Niklaus lifts his hand and pulls my brown hair over my shoulder and brings it up to his face. I can hear him breathing in its scent and rubbing the strands over his cheek. It seems odd to me how and why he does this, but I let him have his moment. It could be worse; his behaviour around me used to be more presumptuous.

Once he was so brazen I pushed him off me, slapped him hard across the face then ran away crying. After that incident he disappeared for many months, possibly a year, and I was lonely; I hadn't realised that Niklaus was my only company. I used to try to keep spirits with me after I pulled them from their bodies, but I couldn't keep them with me for long. Once they see their afterlife they don't acknowledge me, I guess I cease existing for them.

When Niklaus left me here alone for several months I started following nurses around, trying to figure out what was going on. Occasionally I would hear that distinctive 'ting' and found myself being drawn towards the sound. Always it led to someone needing help to leave their body behind. One night I was hurrying after a bustling nurse and when I turned a corner Niklaus was standing there, leaning against a wall, looking down at his shoe, but taking furtive glances towards me. A surge of emotion rushed from my heart to my head and every part of my body as I hurried over and hugged him, basking in the comfort of not being alone. The resentment I felt toward him for the presumptuous grappling momentarily forgotten because of the torture of being surrounded by people who won't acknowledge me. Even his presence is preferable to nothing.

When I hugged him Niklaus was a little shocked, but after a beat he put his arms around me and apologised. He said he'd been alone for a long time and just wanted to be close to someone. I told him I hated him, but I needed him to keep me sane. He accepted that and promised he'd keep himself restrained so long as there was common ground between us. From then on we would talk and I'd let him touch my hair, any skin that's exposed in what I'm wearing, and kiss my cheek sometimes when we part. I don't know where he goes. I assume he has to go and help a spirit from its body. I don't know why he can leave and I can't.

I still have to fend off Niklaus's advances occasionally. He'll try and push the boundaries of our relationship further, and I know it's not enough for him. But I shrug him off and he stops.

"Happy enough," I say as I snap my mind back into the present. "I suppose they were happy enough. You can't assume that Michael and Mary were soul mates, they could have grown out of their infatuation once they were older."

Niklaus drops my hair and I turn to face him, though my eyes don't meet his. "Why do you know how Mary died?" I ask.

Niklaus lifts his hand and tilts my chin so my green eyes meet his dark brown ones. "I just do," he replies. He lifts the other to cup my face in his hands; I allow this gesture but say, "Please don't try..."

"I'm not!" he hisses.

I can see in his face that I've offended him. He hasn't tried anything in ages, so I try to relax. I close my eyes and feel his hands on my cheeks. I must admit I'm enjoying the contact. One of his hands moves through my hair, from the scalp down through to the strands. When he reaches the end I feel his hand move to my shoulder. I'm struggling against opening my eyes. I want to trust him. I'm certain I sense him closer to me. My eyes fling open but I stay still as I feel his lips brushing my cheek, he lingers for a moment then straightens up, dropping his hands to his side.

"Do you hear it like a voice in your head?"

"Hear what?" he replies.

"How they die. Is it like a voice in your head, or do you read it from a book?"

Niklaus looks over my shoulder. I turn my head and see he's looking at the clock. "It's dawn. Do you want to go up to the roof to watch the sunrise?" he asks.

"You haven't answered my question."

"Come up to the roof." Niklaus begins to walk a little down the corridor toward the lift.

I call after him, "If I follow you up to the roof will you answer my question?"

Niklaus turns around and smiles. "Maybe."

I have nothing else to do except follow around another nurse, which I can do any time. Plus Niklaus's visits can be few and far between, so I should take advantage of the social interaction while it's available. I catch up with him at the lift. He's standing behind an orderly who is leaning on a cart. The doors slide open and we follow the orderly in. The orderly hums a tune as he straightens up then pulls his bunched up underwear out of his arse crack. I smile to myself and restrain a giggle – the things people do when they think they're alone. I look at Niklaus and he's looking straight ahead, not paying attention. The door opens at the second highest level; we'll have to take the stairs the rest of the way. We walk out of the lift and walk through the closed door for the stairs. The door to the roof is ajar with a brick for the staff and, occasionally, patients, who come up here to have a cigarette.

There are a few empty milk crates brought up from the kitchen by the staff and a small table stolen from a waiting room. A resident in scrubs has his head in one hand and a lit cigarette in the other. The sky is dark blue and the few clouds that float around glow with a purple haze because the sun hasn't peeked over the horizon yet. I walk over to the edge of the building and lean against the brick. Niklaus does the same. I'm aware it's cold but I don't feel cold like I used to. I don't need to wear my black coat, but I do. The silence is making me uneasy.

"Beautiful isn't it?" I say to Niklaus.

"I've seen the sun rise and fall a hundred thousand times, yet there is still so much beauty in it." Niklaus rests his chin on the heel of his hand nonchalantly.

I wonder if I'll have to ask him my question again and break the serenity.

"I just know." Niklaus says without my further enquiry. "I don't hear voices in my head, I don't read a book. I look at them and I know. Sometimes I see it."

"See it? Like a vision?"

"Sometimes. Other times it's like fragments; key moments about the death, little flashes, bits of a scene."

"I don't get to see that." I say.

"I know." Niklaus replies.

"Why?"

Niklaus turns his back on the sunrise and leans against the brick. "Because you don't want to..." he says.

"Sometimes I do, sometimes I'm curious. There're a lot of things I don't know."

"Such as?"

"Such as my name, I don't even know my name, what I look like, or even what year it is. I think time moves differently for me. Does time move differently for you?"

"You don't know your name?"

"Seriously, out of everything I just said, that's what you took away?"

"But it's your name; it isn't something that is easily forgotten. Can you remember anything before you were here?"

"I remember waking here but not much before." Part of me hopes that Niklaus will give some insight but instead he remains silent. Perhaps he doesn't know either, so I continue in the hope he will give me some tit bit of information.

"Niklaus, I don't know how long I've been here. I can't keep track of time without concentrating. I look out of the window and it's light out and I watch the nurses as they move through the wards and tend to patients, then I find myself looking out the window again and it's pitch black and the nurses are gone. It's quite a strange occurrence; could have sworn I only look away from the window for a minute or two. I don't like how time slips away from me like that. Do you have any idea how that feels?"

Niklaus is looking at the gravel. He is either ignoring me or contemplating what I'm saying, I'm never sure which. Niklaus looks up at me. This is the most I've ever divulged to him and he looks quizzical.

"I do know how that feels, but it would take too long to answer your questions and I don't have that kind of time. Besides, why should I? You seem to be doing fine by yourself and I receive no reward for helping you."

"But I feel like it's out of my control. It's as if my nature takes over and I can't stop what I'm doing. Isn't helping me to understand my existence reward enough?"

In the brightening light of the morning sky I see Niklaus's eyebrows arch in thought as he moves directly in front of me. "Is this why you reject me?"

I'm in a state of confusion. What does he mean? He continues. "You reject me and my affection because your feelings are the only thing you have control over?"

"What?" I am beyond confusion. "No! How did you come to that conclusion? Besides, when on Earth did this conversation become about you? I rejected you because one of my very first memories of you was waking up in this state with your hand pushing up my dress so your fingers could unhook my stockings!"

I draw a deep breath and am on the brink of tears at the sudden recollection of this memory. "The very first moment I met you, I screamed. I woke up on the cold ground with people bustling around me and a strange man trying to undress me and nobody heard me scream. Nobody came to help me when you grabbed my wrists and dragged me down the corridor. I screamed and cried hysterically and people walked on by."

There is complete silence. All I hear is a gust of wind. I don't look at him; I don't want to.

"I tried to explain. I tried to comfort you like I'd seen others do," he whispered.

You tried to kiss me and hold me down! You – the man who was undressing me!"

"I'm sorry that's not what I was trying to do!"

"Then explain it! What possible reason do you have to explain what you did?"

All this tension seems to have been built up for decades. "It was the way you fell..." he says.

I look up at him, into his eyes. They are sad, remorseful.

"You fell on the ground unconscious and your dress was like that. The top of your stocking and suspender was showing; I was curious. I could see your naked skin. Something came over me and I just wanted to know how it felt to have your skin against mine, so I unhooked it. Then you woke up and saw me. You just kept screaming so I pulled you away and tried to comfort you. I'm sorry."

I'm not ready to forgive him, but I see he is remorseful. Perhaps enough to give me a little information, if I ask nicely.

"So, if you don't know my name, you could at least tell me what I look like. I've been in the bathrooms here and stared into the mirrors, but all I see is a hazy outline but there's not defined features, nothing I can recognise or focus on. I know I've got brown hair because it's long, but otherwise..."

Niklaus moves towards me, looking intently at my features.

"Your hair isn't brown. Brown is ordinary, dull. Your hair's the colour of a chestnut mare in the summer sunshine. It's not curly or straight, but has soft waves that bounce around when you walk, and shines brilliantly when the light catches it. Your eyes are a green with flecks of yellow and brown in them. Your lashes are dark and thick, like your hair. Your skin is smooth and pale, and your cheekbones sit high on your face.

I don't see you smile very often, but when you do I see small even teeth around small, pale lips. It's a nice face – symmetrical, actually quite beautiful. There. Does that help? Am I forgiven?"

I absorb this precious information, but say nothing. I just look at him. He is still close but not touching me. The intensity of his gaze fades and his face is morphed into a shadow of sadness.

"You're never going to love me, are you?"

"I'm sorry Niklaus." I turn away. I can't look at the sadness in his eyes when I say it. I still feel resentful towards him, but after listening to his side of the story of my first memory of him, I now have a skerrick of sympathy for his feelings. If I'm feeling trapped and isolated in whatever plane this is, I'm sure he's feeling just as alone as I am.

"Don't do that!" Niklaus takes a step back. "Don't pity me!"

"I'm not, I just... I just... I'm confused," I turn back to look at him, except he isn't there. I walk across the rooftop

"Niklaus!" I scream, but there is no answer; just an eerie silence. "Niklaus, get back here!" I yell into the wind. "We're not done yet!"

I spin in a circle, looking for him. All I see is a desolate rooftop and a guy in scrubs grinding out a cigarette butt.

CHAPTER 3

The sun is up and I am boiling over with emotions. I don't know whether I want to scream or cry. So I do neither. I just stomp toward the door. The young resident is gone but his cigarettes aren't. I remember that I used to smoke!

Red lips kiss the gold filter of a cigarette. A flick of the lighter and a small puff to light the tip of the cigarette, then the smoky wisps of tobacco fill the air. I can't remember when or where I was but the action of smoking is all too familiar.

I sit on the overturned milk crate. My hand withdraws a cigarette from the open packet and I flick open the lighter left there by the doctor, exposing the flint wheel and wick. A few firm strokes of the thumb and the flame springs to life.

I breathe deeply and taste the tobacco on my tongue. Its soothing tendrils seeking out every crevice and pocket within my lungs, soothing my nerves as the nicotine hits my brain. Why have I not tried this sooner? I lift the cigarette to my lips again and a draw deep. Closing my eyes, I drift as I exhale. My fingers examine the lighter. It is cold and heavy. I look down and see it is beaten with age. One side, crudely scratched into the steel, I read: 'Live today to die tomorrow'. The other side has the initials 'ER' in beautifully formed script.

A flicker of a memory envelopes my mind. My hair pulled back under a starched cap. A man, in his mid-twenties, with red-dish brown hair, lighting my cigarette. I lean into the flame, "Thank you. That's an unusual lighter."

"It was my father's when he was in the war." The man lights his own cigarette and the memory is gone.

I've seen this lighter before...

I hear the rooftop door open. I stand and see Margie and the young brunette nurse approaching. The cigarette, still lit, and lighter fall though my hands onto the gravel as they draw closer to me. I attempt to snuff the cigarette out in the gravel, but my attempt fails.

"Dr Reeves must have been up here already this morning. These are his brand of cigarettes," the young brunette says.

"You'll have to return them to him later, Nicole."

Margie sees the lighter by my foot, bends down and picks it up. She's face to face with me and I don't move, I just stare at her face. My gosh – she's gotten old, when did those lines around her mouth happen?

"His lighter is here too." Margie hands it to Nicole. "He'll appreciate you giving them back to him, rather than some old woman like me."

"Oh Margie, you're not old yet!" Nicole lights her cigarette with the old beaten lighter, then continues the conversation. "Dr Reeves is really cute. Have you noticed how much weight he's lost since he started here?"

"They always do; they eat nothing but junk when they're studying, then once they start their residency, they never have time to eat," Margie replies with a small chuckle.

"Margie, do you think I should lean right over his desk when I give him back his lighter?" Nicole has both her hands palm down on the small table. I can see right down her top, which means so can Margie. I look at Nicole disapprovingly, which might be effective if she could see me.

"Oh Nicole, in my day women didn't chase men! We let them do the chasing. Although, it was during the war, so a few of the girls let their morals slip. My best friend at the time chased after a doctor, even though he wasn't free. She caught him alright, but it didn't end well."

"Why? What happened? Was he married?"

Margie has a faraway look in her eye. "Yes, he was, but there was more to it than that".

Nicole sees a look of pain and sadness in Margie's face and shifts gears.

"Well, whatever it was, it isn't going to happen to me. At this point I'm only in it for fun. We're always cooped up in this hospital – I enjoy a bit of harmless flirting. And if Dr Gorgeous wants to screw around a little, I'd be up for that," Nicole says in a breathy, sensual voice as she shimmies her shoulders towards Margie.

"So long as you know what you're doing," Margie sighs and draws on her cigarette.

"Course I do! I've got it all worked out."

Nicole's mildly irritating display is distracting me from my recent conversation with Niklaus, so I move towards and through the door just as Nicole starts to reply. As I head down the stairs I reflect on my conversation with Niklaus and realise I didn't learn much about my existence. I wonder if Niklaus is keeping information from me intentionally, and if so why? Perhaps I haven't been open enough to let him confide in me. In order to talk, there needs to be trust, but I doubt if I'll ever be able to trust him. I stop mid-step and take a deep breath; this is only frustrating me. I need a distraction. One more flight and I'm on level five. I jump the last three steps like a small child and walk through the closed door into the maternity ward.

When the strain of helping people pass on becomes overwhelming, I like to come here and gaze at the newborns. This ward is always full of new life and reminds me that these babies can't live if others don't die. I'm facilitating the circle of life, even though I don't enjoy it. I walk past the brightly painted mural that's been there for decades. Children's smudgy hand prints form a colourful border around a flattened world map, with a ribboned scroll draped across the top that reads 'Hope for a better generation' in large blue and pink script. I've always thought it was ugly and wish they'd paint over it. Who says one generation is better than the other? Every generation has its own troubles and varying degrees of prosperity.

I walk straight past the nurses' station towards the viewing room. Usually, the babies will be up and active at this hour, all going crazy for food and attention at once. The exhausted nurses will be run off their feet and it's delightful to watch. I sit on the bench in front of the large glass window and watch the early morning drama unfold. I do find it amusing – you'd think after all this time they would have organised a more thorough routine. All the little babies are wrapped tight in their blankets, their sleeping faces pinched in little twitching expressions, lost in their little baby dreams. The only maternity nurse in the ward is tending to a premature baby in an incubator.

When this ward was updated a few years ago I spent a lot of time here. They sent specialised nurses to train the maternity staff, and I sat in on the lectures when I could. I found it fascinating.

I see one of the babies stir and stretch against its cocoon. Soon it'll start crying and then the rest will follow. Once one wakes it's a domino effect.

"Dr Reeves? Are you OK?" The voice behind me comes from a dark-skinned woman in pale yellow scrubs. I follow her eye line: Dr Reeves is sitting on the bench in a white coat and blue scrubs.

"Sixteen hours on shift, fourteen more to go." Dr Reeves weakly smiles at the nurse.

She nods in sympathy. "When are you back on the floor?"

"I'm on-call for three more hours," Reeves holds his head in his hands and runs his fingers through his coppery hair and exhales. I step closer to Reeves and crouch down to be level with his face. His skin is oily and face unshaven. His eyes are blood-shot and bleary, and he has a long way to go before the end of his shift. I don't understand why all the young nurses drool over him. Sure, he has a nice face and body, but he always looks drained as he shuffles around the wards. Perhaps he is handsome in his everyday life – out of scrubs and laughing with his friends in the fresh air and sunlight. I only get to see him under harsh fluorescent lights when he's pushed to the limit.

The nurse moves to him and put a hand on his shoulder. Reeves lifts his head and looks at her.

"Why don't you go take a shower and change your scrubs? You'll feel better. Then try and get a little sleep. We'll wake you if we need you."

Reeves mutters his thanks as the first baby's wail wakes the others and sets off the anticipated chain reaction. The nurse moves towards the viewing room as Reeves straightens up and walks right through me toward the lift. I hesitate for a moment, weighing up the relative merits of this morning's entertainment – I follow him. The lift doors open and a man with a worried expression exits with a bouquet of daffodils. I get on just as the door closes. Reeves presses floor one and leans against the lift wall. He draws a deep breath that turns into a wide yawn. I sense a whiff of stale coffee and cigarettes that takes me to a distant memory that I can hardly grasp: a man holding my face and bending in for a kiss; that same scent on his breath mingled with faded aftershave. I didn't mind the combination – it was comforting, sensual. But I can't quite get a grip on those memories; it's like trying to recall a dream after waking. Everything's faded. Memories, sensations – my perception of smell is so muted now; small particles seem to filter through the veil, but the invisible wall between our worlds stands strong, separating all the sensations and giving my life a dull numbness.

The lift dings and the doors open. At the end of another corridor Reeves swipes his access card to enter the doctors' mess. The mess is well named. It's rarely clean; there are always dirty dishes in the sink, and spilled coffee on the table. I stand in the middle of the room and look around. One scrawny young man sits upright, sleeping, and unaware that he is snoring loudly. A rounded woman gobbles a large meal while skimming a magazine. Reeves gives the woman a silent nod as he walks past, which she absentmindedly returns. He walks to the empty coffee pot, rinses out the jug and puts fresh grounds into a new filter. I watch him switch it on then head to the lockers. He retrieves his backpack and some fresh green scrubs and enters the men's bathrooms. I follow him in.

Reeves throws his backpack onto a wooden bench that is attached to a blue tiled wall. He unzips the bag and removes a toiletries bag, towel and socks. I stand in the corner of the room out of his way – I don't enjoy being walked through. Lethargically, Reeves removes his coat, placing it on a wall hanger. He throws his scrubs into the corner I'm standing in. When he's down to his underwear I consider turning my back to give him privacy. Though, the benefits of invisibility are that modesty is no longer an issue. I have screamed into people's ear and provoked little response; nobody knows that I'm here except for Niklaus. I look over Reeves's body; he isn't muscular but he is smoothly toned apart from a little softness around his belly that I find strangely endearing. His skin is smooth and lightly sprinkled with freckles on his arms and shoulders. The weight Reeves has lost during long hours at the hospital suits him – he now has a strong jawline where his rounded face and soft chin were. As Reeves bends to remove his jocks he turns his back to me, which robs me of a full frontal view but offers the opportunity to check out his firm backside and I wonder if he's been working out lately. I feel my cheeks flush as I realise how inappropriate I'm being. If I were visible I would never ogle a man so overtly. Once I hear the water begin to run behind the half wall I move over to the bench and sit. I close my eyes and rest my head against the tiles. I never sleep, but I do enjoy having these quiet moments to think of nothing. There are few silent places in a hospital. When I sit in the chapel I feel like I don't belong, and it's creepy and clichéd when I hang out in the morgue. The water drowns out any other sounds, it's relaxing...

"I lost a patient today." My eyes fling open and turn to the sound; it's behind the half wall. "I lost a patient today and it's my fault."

I move towards the sound of his voice and peep behind the wall. The steam is heavy but I can see Reeves sitting on the tiled floor under the hot water that cascades over his back and head. His finger dig into his scalp as he rubs his hands through his hair. He looks down at the tiles in anguish. I lean against the opposite wall and slide my back down it until I'm sitting on the floor with him. "I'm so tired, I keep making mistakes," Reeves whispers to himself.

Reeves picks up a wash cloth and lathers it up with a bar of soap. He washes himself while sitting on the floor then mechanically scrubs his teeth. I get up and leave the bathroom as the water cuts out. I walk through the door of the on-call room where I hope Reeves will come to sleep. I notice the bed is unmade and dishevelled, and probably used by other exhausted medical staff. Cleaners obviously haven't been in yet. It's not often I intervene, but I find myself locking the door, then pulling out a fresh fitted sheet and pillow case from the cupboard in the room. Pushing through the veil takes physical effort, but the mechanics of stripping a bed and making it are something I feel I've been trained to do. I throw the dirty bedding into the hamper as the door knob jiggles. I release the lock and Reeves staggers through the door and collapses on the freshly made bed. I remember my mother always said, "you never sleep better than on clean starched sheets." I hope that holds true for the doctor's sake. I leave him be and continue my wandering.

CHAPTER 4

It's mid-morning and the foyer has begun to fill up with people waiting for appointments with specialists. This hospital isn't an overly large one and most of the work done here is private. I walk into the hospital grounds, the sun is up and it's warm outside. I breathe deeply and I'm certain I can smell a vague scent of spring. There are two main buildings here; the first was built of stone in the late 1800s, and was converted into a high care facility after the larger modern facility was completed. The stable, long-term coma patients still remain in the old hospital, but they've been relocated to the basement in a makeshift coma ward. I was around when the staff debated moving them across to the new building, but it was decided they didn't need windows, so it was agreed it was unnecessary to move them.

I always see this ward as human storage for broken equipment. The staff duties here are limited to patient care, pressure area checks, and equipment monitoring. There's never more than one nurse and an assistant on duty here at any time, and they don't hang around. Mostly they sit in the nurses' station chatting or flicking through magazines while their patients lie in silent death-like slumbers. I worry that one of them will wake here, and be plunged into a different and unfamiliar world to the one they've left. Even though the ward is in the basement, it isn't dirty and dank down here – the walls are cream coloured and the rooms are flooded with fluorescent lighting. Without windows, it's easy to lose a sense of time here. I can wander through the narrow hall here with both arms stretched wide, running my fingertips along the walls without fear of someone walking through me. Towards the end of the corridor is an open door that I walk through into a familiar room that contains three beds, each with its own rail and curtains that I've never seen drawn. The patients here don't have a concept of time passing, which makes a mockery of the round, plastic clock on the wall, with its large hands and audible tick. In each bed an unconscious man is hooked up to monitoring equipment and fluid bags. I visit them regularly, but I still sense that none of them are ready to die, which I feel is sad – they are all stable, but absent from reality.

I walk over to the first bed; a chair is already placed beside the bed from when last I visited. I wonder if the nurses ever notice the furniture has moved. An elderly man lies there, breathing serenely, looking as if he's just sleeping. "Hello, Albert." I don't know if that's his real name as he's been in a coma for years, but I can't bring myself to call him 'John Doe'.

"It's nice to see you. It's been a strange day for me. Niklaus visited this morning, and we watched the sunrise together which was nice, I guess. I really want some answers and I'm not sure how to get them from him. You know he doesn't usually stay here for very long, which can be frustrating. I did my best to open up to him but it didn't get me very far. He's not telling me what I want to know." I sit in silence and let the peaceful ambiance absorb me for a moment.

"Dr Reeves is still exhausted. He hardly sleeps between his shifts. He's not coping as well as some of the other doctors are with the back-to-back shifts. Nicole is still infatuated with him. She's found an excuse to talk to him, but she hasn't used it yet." I lean into the hard back of the hospital chair and take a deep breath then let it out slowly. The tick of the ward clock echoes loudly in this under-furnished room. The rhythmic tick-tock is mesmerising, measuring seconds in slow motion and making me feel almost hypnotised.

"My whole existence is weird. It's a bit like yours, Albert. We don't really understand why we're here, but we're stuck. Kinda sucks – as Nicole would say."

I know he can't respond, which is fine. I just want to feel like I have a connection with someone. Someone I can share my experience with, and pretend he's listening.

TING!

"I've got to go Albert, but I'll be back soon to visit." I smile at him, but of course, I receive no response.

TING!

I rise from my chair, close my eyes and let the bell pull me out of this room and into another...

CHAPTER 5

I find myself standing in the level four ladies bathrooms. Someone is vomiting in one of the stalls. It looks like this might take a while. I pull myself up onto the vanity bench and lean my head against the mirror. The woman retches again and then there is silence. I sit and wait.

The cubicle door flicks across to 'vacant' and I lift my head to see a gaunt-looking woman stagger out of the stall to clutch at the sink. There are a few tufts of sparse hair left on her head and her skin is dry and brittle. I watch as she rinses out her mouth and splashes her face. From a small clutch purse she pulls out a white prescription bottle, struggles with the cap and swallows down six pills with a drink of water from the faucet. The woman shuffles out of the bathroom. I sigh and look around, I get down off the bench and kick open every stall. Nobody else is here; she must be who I'm here for.

I walk out of the bathroom and follow the woman into a semi private chemo infusion room. She gingerly sits down in a recliner and the nurse hooks up her treatment to her port.

"Is there anything I can get for you, Marylyn?" The nurse asks after taping down her IV.

"Some water please?" The woman's frail voice rasps. "I forgot my medication."

The nurse smiles and pours the woman a cup of water from the jug nearby. Marylyn fishes out the white prescription bottle again and attempts to open the bottle.

"Would you like some help there, Marylyn?"

"No, no thank you." The bottle clicks open. Marylyn shakes three pills out of the bottle onto her palm, then closes the lid and places the bottle back into her handbag.

The nurse passes the cup and Marylyn swallows the pills.

"Thank you," Marylyn gives the nurse a weak smile.

The nurse gently squeezes Marylyn's forearm and moves to the next patient. There's a caregivers chair in the corner. I sit and wait. It doesn't take long before Marylyn clears her throat, and looks at me. Not through me, but at me.

"Hi! Can you see me?" It always gives me a boost when someone acknowledges me, and have to remind myself that these are this woman's last moments.

"Who are you?" Marylyn asks.

"Oh, I'm just here to help you transition. You're Marylyn, right?"

The woman blinks lazily a few times and weakly nods. "What are you waiting for then?"

"You're not close enough to death yet. You could still be saved."

"I don't want to be saved."

"Too bad – I don't like doing this, and it can be avoided if you're saved, so I'll wait till the very last moment." I realise I'm speaking a little too casually.

There is silence for a moment then Marylyn holds back tears and mutters. "I'm tired. I'm in pain all the time. Even if I do beat this cancer I'll never be the same. Chemo kills too many healthy cells." A tear rolls down Marylyn's emaciated cheek.

For a long moment I look at the desperate spirit trapped within the failing body, and think over what she has just said. "Why here?" I ask. "A hospital isn't the best place to commit suicide."

"I live alone. I have no family. I don't want my friends to find my body." Marylyn coughs, and then drinks a little more water to clear her throat.

Good answer, I think to myself. I stand and walk over to Marylyn. I kneel at her feet and Marylyn leans forward.

"I never imagined Death would look like you, if I imagined it at all. You're so young and beautiful..."

I can't smile at her compliment, because it feels inappropriate, but I whisper my thanks.

"My hair use to be long and wavy like yours, I dyed it bright pink before I started chemo." Marylyn chuckles to herself and I can't help but smile.

Our eyes meet and she knows it's time. I place both my hands over hers and pull Marylyn's spirit gently out of her body. Marylyn looks the wasted body in the recliner and reaches out to it. Her hands are smooth now and her skin fine. She rotates them slowly in front of her face, then runs them through her long blonde hair. She draws a delighted sharp breath as her hands clutch her full cheeks and she grins at me.

"Thank you," Marylyn says as she closes her eyes and lifts her arms upward as her spirit swirls into a ball of warm golden light and ascends through the ceiling. I think that's the first time in all my years doing this job that I've been thanked. "You're welcome!" I call up to the ceiling. That woman sure knows how to make an exit.

The body in the recliner is already cold and the eyes stare blankly into nothingness. I push through the veil to pull down her eyelids with my fingertips. Now it simply looks as though she's sleeping peacefully. I'm a little sad that she didn't try to save herself by coughing up the pills at the last moment, but I can only hope that she's at peace now. The nurse approaches and attempts to rouse her patient. I leave the ward as I hear the nurse calling Marylyn's name, then calling for a doctor.

Hmm... I wonder what Margie's doing? I wander down to the ICU looking for her, but I can't see her anywhere. The clock on the wall tells me it's almost 8:00pm, so Margie might have finished her shift already. I walk through the double doors into Emergency looking for something to entertain me. I spot Margie talking to Nicole at the nurses' station, but I grimace when I see that Margie has her coat on and her handbag on her shoulder. I look over towards Reeves who's still soldiering on, looking a little fresher, so he must have gotten his second wind knowing his gruelling shift is almost over. He scribbles on a script pad for a patient and signs off to have them discharged, then he walks through the ER to the nurses' station.

"Is Dr Matthews on the floor yet?" Reeves asks.

"Yeah, I saw her take a patient file ten minutes ago." A rounded middle aged nurse replies with a smile.

"Thanks Susie. Ok ladies, I'm off now. Have a good night."

The nurses wave a friendly goodnight, as Reeves and I take the lift to level one. He retrieves his backpack from the doctors' mess, opens it up and rummages around for something. His brow crinkles in consternation, so I follow him to his office.

Reeves's office isn't much bigger than a cupboard and is hardly ever used. The majority of his time is spent in the ER or ICU. He opens one of the top draws of his desk, as there's a rap at the door. Nicole is leaning against the door frame.

"Dr Reeves..." Her voice is soft and sultry.

She sashays to his desk and leans over, far more forward than necessary in my opinion. She places the cigarettes and the old lighter on the desk and slides it towards him.

"I found these on the rooftop. I'm pretty sure they're yours." Nicole straightens her back but keeps her chest pushed forward.

"Thank you. I was just looking for them." Reeves smiles with relief.

"You're welcome, Doctor. I'm about to go up to the roof for a smoke. Do you want to join me?"

Reeves glances at his watch. "Don't you have to go back on the floor?"

Nicole shakes her head. "I'm finished for the night. I've been waiting for you. I wanted to give back your things."

"Oh. Ok, thanks." Reeves puts down his backpack and escorts Nicole out of the room, his hand guiding her at the waist. Nicole looks up at him with a suggestive smile.

I follow them up to the roof top. They walk over to the edge of the building and lean against the brick wall. Reeves leans in to light Nicole's cigarette, then ignites his own. I catch up with them as their faces are illuminated in the brief flicker of light, and hear their conversation.

"It looks like you had a hard day today..." Nicole's voice is drenched with compassion, and I groan loudly.

"Yeah, it was a long stretch. One of the surgeons called in sick, so I had to work a triple shift."

"When do you have to be back?" Nicole asks, looking like she's just making conversation.

"Fifteen hours and counting. It takes me an hour and a half just to get home." Reeves said.

"Oh, you poor thing..." Nicole's voice is dripping with sympathy, and I know exactly where she's heading. "I only live fifteen minutes away. You could stay at my apartment if you like."

"I wouldn't like to impose."

"Actually, you'd be helping me. I don't like taking the train home alone this late at night."

Reeves shifts his weight from one foot to the other and looks out to the city skyline. He brings his cigarette to his mouth for a long drag before answering.

"If we leave together people will talk," his voice is husky with uncertainty.

"Well, I don't care if they talk." Nicole says with a cavalier attitude. "Would you be embarrassed being seen leaving with me?"

"Oh! No, I wouldn't... You're very attractive. I ah... wouldn't be embarrassed, no."

Reeves looks away from Nicole and I'm certain he's blushing!

Nicole waits for a moment then says. "So, are you coming home with me?"

"Well, yes, thanks, so long as you don't mind."

"No, of course not. But I should tell you, I've only got the one bed."

"Oh, I see. Nicole, are you asking me if I want to... with you?"

Nicole giggles. "Honestly Doctor, it's like you've never had anyone hit on you before."

"Ah well, it's been a while and ah..."

I've never seen Reeves so bashful before, even in the darkness I tell he's struggling with this situation.

"I've been dropping hints for a while, you've been so consumed by your work I don't think you look at any of us nurses as women at all do you? You're not batting for the other team, are you?" Nicole teases him gently.

"Oh, of course I like women; but you're right about me being focused on my work." Reeves manages to say, and I almost feel sorry for him; Nicole has found her prey and has cornered it.

Nicole pushes in front of Reeves and puts her arms around his neck, pressing her body against his. Reeves doesn't resist, and after a sigh of acquiescence finds his hands are smoothing over her hips, then pulling her body towards his into a lingering hug. It looks to me like he hasn't held anyone in a long while. He savours the moment and the exhaustion melts away from his face.

Nicole seems to feel his body relax and takes the opportunity to tilt her head up to his, brushing her lips along the edge of his mouth. Reeves kisses her lips softly, clearly enjoying the sensation of her warm breath on his skin. Nicole's hands find Reeves' buttocks and she squeezes them, uttering a low murmur. She intensifies the kiss, devouring his mouth with gusto. I feel a little awkward just standing here watching. Then I remind myself that I get so little amusement, and this is as good as it gets.

I watch as the two finally break from a lengthy kiss, Reeves runs his hand around Nicole's waist and pulls her tighter to him. He moves his hand to her cheek and kisses her again deeply.

Whoa, Reeves knows what he's doing when he's locking lips. Lucky Nicole.

He breaks the kiss again. "Sorry, I got a little carried away... it's been a little while for me." Reeves strokes her cheek with his thumb.

"No need to apologise – that was intense, but good. It feels like you're ready to come home with me..." Nicole replies as she runs her hands up Reeves' thighs.

Reeves' face is flushed – I can't tell if it's from arousal, or if he's just not used to women approaching him so assertively.

Nicole pulls Reeves away from the brick ledge and kisses him again briefly. Reeves leans in for more, but she puts her palm flat on his chest.

"Did you drive in?" Nicole asks. Reeves just nods and with that Nicole leads Reeves off the rooftop. I stay where I am and think about those two. I feel a begrudging admiration for Nicole and the way she handled the situation. She seems to have Reeves wrapped around her little finger. I wish I could remember if I ever had the power to seduce a man like that. I half hope she has real feelings for him. Maybe the reason Reeves focuses solely on work is because he has no significant other in his life.

I feel it before I hear it – a faint TING!

I gather my thoughts together and follow the sound of the torturous TING!

CHAPTER 6

I close my eyes and everything fades to black. When I open my eyes I'm in the car park out the front of the hospital. I'm standing in a pool of light, one of the many security lights that illuminate the gardens and pathways to the staff car park. There are a dozen or so cars waiting here in the semi-darkness, but I can't see any people. I close my eyes once more and search the area for my calling; it's faint, dropping on and off my internal radar, but it begins to pull me towards a small weather-beaten blue car with subtle hints of rust. I peer through the windows and see piles of food wrappers and papers littering the front dashboard. In the backseat, in addition to bundles of clothing, is a small toddler strapped into a car seat and sleeping peacefully. I grimace at what I see in the front seat – a thin young woman wearing a distressed pair of jeans and a black singlet has a makeshift tourniquet around her upper arm and a drowsy expression on her face. With marks up her arms and a needle close by I can barely see her chest rise and fall. I know she's breathing because her slumped head is against the window and her breath is fogging up the glass slightly with every depressed breath she manages to take. As I watch, the fog patch grows smaller and smaller until it finally ceases entirely. I reach through the glass pane and into her chest pulling from it a loud screeching soul that looks to be made of shattered glass.

"Am I dead?" She grabs my shoulders and shakes me desperately.

"Ye... ye...yes," I manage to say, thrown off guard by never having been approached by a soul in such a state.

"Yes! Yes! Finally it's over." The woman starts to sob, though I'm unsure whether these are tears of sadness or joy.

"Gr... um... great." I'm so confused. I don't want to offend the recently deceased.

Though the soul is shattered, it has a faint gold aura around it.

"Am I broken?"

"Yes," I reply.

The soul seems distressed and looks at her hands, assessing the damage "Oh no," she mutters. "It'll take lifetimes to repair what's been done."

While I had seen 'broken' souls before, most had looked like a fracture in glass, and the majority didn't seem to mind, while others hadn't noticed these imperfections at all. This woman seems more self-aware than any other I've met. I don't know what creates these fractures, but they seem to occur often in war veterans and concentration camp survivors. Maybe trauma, pain and suffering leads to these fractures? I've seen some souls with barely visible cracks – a fixed seam in their soul where their wounds had healed. I've never seen any damage as extensive as in this woman's soul, which surprises me since her soul seems so young.

The golden soul touches her stomach, "I'm pregnant, well at least she was."

"You don't see yourself as her?" I grab the opportunity to speak with an entity that seems self-aware. Maybe I'll get some answers about what's going on?

"No. Every day she abused her body, and every day I'd scream in agony as another fracture was made." The soul looks back at her lifeless body. "I think the baby's soul is the only thing holding me together. New life."

A bright light appears and out steps a tall slender woman, she seems to be in her early 40s, and wears jeans and a plaid shirt.

"Mum?" the golden soul says, as tears well up in her eyes.

The older woman smiles and holds out her arms.

The shattered golden soul walks straight into the woman's arms and the woman encompasses her. "I'm sorry I left you so soon. I watched you and saw everything you endured. It wasn't supposed to be like that. I thought he was a good man, someone who'd take care of my children."

"It's not your fault. He was good in the beginning and then it all started going wrong. Look what's happened to me Mum! I'm broken." The golden soul cries as she holds tight to her mother.

"It's all right, the baby will protect you from shattering. You'll fuse with it and hopefully begin again after spending some time on the other side."

The light brightens, like when mercury is set on fire, then blazes and disappears in an instant. Inside the car the toddler wakes and begins to scream, as if it knew its mother was gone from this plane.

I walk away from the scene towards the hospital. Dr Reeves and Nicole are making their way to the car park, trailed by another nurse finishing her shift. It won't be long before someone finds the toddler. A car has already backed out of its space, with Reeves in the driver's seat and Nicole beside him. Behind me I hear a woman shouting for help, and a man runs through me towards her and the weather-beaten rust bucket.

CHAPTER 7

When I get into the building, Dr Matthews is assessing a barely conscious young woman who is splayed across a trolley bed. Her two friends who brought her into Emergency look on with glazed panda eyes. Their strappy dresses battle to contain their breasts and barely cover their legs. They both look like the evening has taken its toll on them too.

"How much has Emma had to drink?" Matthews asks as she scribbles on the girl's chart.

The blonde is leaning against the bed to keep her balance in her red six-inch Jimmy Choo stilettos.

"Not much. She must have like totally had her drink spiked. She usually drinks way more. Right Cassandra?"

"Yeah, way more," Cassandra agrees, nodding her head and chewing gum as she talks.

"What time did she start drinking, and what did she drink?" Matthews asks politely.

"Well, we had a couple of ciders around four this afternoon when the boys came over, then we went out to dinner and shared a bottle of white wine. Then we met up with Cassandra and went to this party and we started doing shots with these guys, Cassandra was like 'Hell no, Jagar is just ick...' but Emma was like crushing on the guy that was pouring them so she had five with him so that she could like, impress him or something..."

"He wasn't even that hot," Cassandra interjected.

"Yeah, I know right? Emma could totally do better, but anyway. So after that we drank a few double bubblegum vodka shooters and like..."

"Ok, Stop." Dr Matthews said.

"Rude much? Like, I wasn't even finished..." the blonde one says.

"We are just trying to, you know, help our friend. She could have been like raped or something worse if we weren't with her." Cassandra said.

"She's drunk," Matthews says.

"No, she usually drinks, like, twice that amount," the blonde one replies.

"Oh my God! Our friend has totally been drugged and you don't even care!" Cassandra pouts.

I burst out into laugher at these ridiculous women. The entertainment value of this hospital just got better.

Matthews strains to continue being polite. "Your friend has drunk enough alcohol to make two men fall down drunk. I've given her fluids and I can do a drug screen if that will help put her mind at ease, though anything she's taken will come up in the screen."

The blonde and Cassandra exchange looks, "No, I'm sure she'll be fine. Thank you," Cassandra says.

Dr Matthews walks away, and under hear breath I hear her say, "Yeah bitch, that's what I thought."

I quite like Dr Matthews; she's clever and is funny at times. Sometimes I have to jog beside her because my short legs can hardly keep up with her long tanned ones. She's quite attractive, but looks somewhat like a boy with her blonde hair cut short, and her loose-fitting clothes hiding her bosom.

I follow Matthews as she tends to two other patients, both routine and nothing of interest to me. Then she comes to a young boy who is looking slightly green and clutching his stomach. Matthews picks up the chart and looks over what's been written. "So... Alex, not feeling very well?" Matthews asks.

"No, it's my tummy. It really hurts," the small child says.

Matthews talks to the mother who says that he hasn't been eating much but that she wasn't concerned because Alex is fussy about his food.

"Does he eat a lot of bread?" asks Matthews, the mother nods.

"I can't get him to eat vegetables or fruit, I've tried everything." The mother is clearly distressed.

Matthews leans down and asks the boy if she can have a look at his 'tummy', and he nods. I can see his abdomen is swollen and hard. Matthews asks Alex to sit up and as he does the boy vomits bile all over Matthews's shirt and pants. I see Matthews roll her eyes and the mother apologises profusely. Matthews smiles her most sincere smile and the little boy apologises and vomits again, Matthews manages to step out of the way in the short few seconds available.

"Nurse!" Matthews calls.

A rotund nurse, Susie, opens the curtain and takes in the mess on Matthews' uniform.

"Nurse, could you please arrange some fluids and an x-ray of Alex's abdomen? I'll be back on the floor shortly; I just need to clean up."

"Certainly Doctor, and I'll arrange an orderly as well to ah, clean up."

In the background the young mother mutters her apologies. Matthews wipes the excess bile off her shoes, shirt and slacks. She heads for the doctor's mess to shower and I stay on her heels.

CHAPTER 8

D r Matthews throws her soiled clothes into the collective linen basket then steps into a shower cubicle. I'm loitering as if I'm keeping a friend company. She's out of the shower in a few minutes, dries quickly and gets straight into fresh scrubs and a clean white coat then leaves the bathroom, no doubt heading back to the ER floor. She's thrown her towel over the wooden bench and left behind her toiletries bag in her rush to leave. I enjoy rifling through the possessions of the living, updating my small collection of pilfered items. I take a tiny bottle of shower gel then notice Matthews hasn't closed her locker properly. I help myself to a fresh pair of white knickers and watch them change to inky black as I drag them through the veil. I don't need to change my clothes, since I don't sweat, but I enjoy trying on different styles, especially as the fashions have changed so much over the decades, and besides, playing dress ups breaks up the monotony.

I don't need to shower either, but I like to. One thing I can remember is I used to love to take long hot showers in the winter when I was alive; I loved the feeling of being clean and smelling fresh. I can't feel the stream of water like before, and the water has to be scalding hot or I can't feel it on my skin, but I like to pretend. I don't bother to wash my hair. I've tried, but it only gets damp like when the clouds sprinkle water before it rains. It's kind of weird actually, like there's an invisible veil that only allows the smallest shimmer of reality to seep through.

I drop my black coat on the bathroom bench and step out of my dark jeans, then stand in front of the mirror and wipe away the stream. The palest of skin, toned curves and long dark brown hair, I pull my dark loose curls into a bun, remove my basic black underwear and step into the shower. I take a deep breath of steam and let my muscles relax. Bliss.

I kneel on the cubicle tiles and close my eyes. I smile at the thoughts that dance in my head, I'm not really here. I'm somewhere else, sitting on a porch, in a light blue cotton dress and smoking a cigarette, feeling the sun against my skin. I'm just happy. Nothing happens in this daydream; it's just nice to be somewhere else. Somewhere that isn't a hospital, forever waiting for a terrible TING! to go off in my head; making me bear witness to yet another death and then to make it worse, I watch them go off into a brilliant light while I stay right where I am. Forever trapped in a recurring loop that is my life, or death, or whatever this is.

I'm crying.

I open my eyes and wipe away a tear and decide I have to get out of here. Out of this hospital, whether it's through the invisible wall that separates me from reality, or through a portal into the afterlife. I can't go on living like this, every day exactly the same routine...

CHAPTER 9

After re-dressing I step out of the bathroom into the mess. The news is playing in the background and on the television screen I see a familiar face! It's the man from room 736 had his blood taken by Margie. I turn to listen to the woman relaying the story:

> ...Harold Barden is to stand trial today over the accusation of the molestation and death of local boy, Ben Thompson, whose body was found under the Samford overpass last November. Judgement proceedings have been adjourned on several occasions due to Barden's ill health, though a ruling should be made now that Mr Barden has been released from St Lucia's Memorial Hospital in a stable condition. On a lighter note a dedication has been made...

"Un-fucking-believable!"

The expletive comes from the direction of Justin; a gawky-looking young man who assists Dr Drac in the pathology lab. That's not his real name, of course, but it's what everybody calls him behind his back. Justin has limited contact with patients and staff apart from Dr Drac, but he speaks candidly with the few co-workers he knows. He's sitting on a suede navy couch in a white lab coat next to Dr Reeves, both of whom are watching the news with their feet up on the coffee table. I swear to God I just saw Reeves leave with Nicole an hour ago but now he's back. Time must have slipped away from me again.

"What?" Reeves looks at Justin.

Justin draws a breath to begin a spiel. ' Well, we fix the pedo up, just so he can live out his now healthy long life in a cell as a burden on us tax payers! It's a waste of fucking money and medication, we shudda let him die. Oi, weren't you the attending on his case?"

Reeves nods. "Trust me there was no opportunity for sabotage or negligence on Barden's case, not with the whole world watching." Reeves stretches his arms above his head and places his hands behind his head.

Justin raises his index finger. "Firstly that's not what I heard. Secondly, I doubt anyone would disapprove – even Barden's family isn't standing by him. Probably realised he was a funny uncle long ago, but nobody said nuffin."

"Even though Barden is a criminal of the worst kind, he still has rights and that includes access to healthcare." There's a moment of silence, then Reeves sighs and turns his head to Justin. "What did you hear?"

Justin pops his head over the couch and looks around the mess, then relaxes back into the chair and continues. "Well I didn't hear nuffin, but, when the blood specimens came in for testing they were severely haemolysed. Procedure states we still have to run the bloods, but the results were all over the place. The Drac said that it looked like someone had done it on purpose..."

I remembered the moment when I watched Margie dropping the plastic vials over and over again on the floor.

Reeves straightens and hisses at Justin. "Why wasn't I told my results were inaccurate? With the wrong results I could have ended up killing a patient!"

Justin's eyes shot up in surprise. "You didn't notice that you received two sets of results for the same patient with the preliminary levels being ridiculous?"

Reeves looked embarrassed.

"Besides, the Drac thought you might have had something to do with it, ya see?" Reeves eyebrows shot up in shock at such an accusation, admittedly so did mine; it was ludicrous. Justin continued. "He sent me up from the lab immediately to do a recollect from the patient after he saw the results."

"That over-educated vamp thinks I endangered my patient's life intentionally?!" Reeves couldn't hide the insult from his voice.

"Well... only limited staff members were allowed into Barden's room due to security. Only you, hospital admin and Margie where allowed in. I had to get a note from Drac to get past the cop at the door"

"So Dr Drac assumes I'm at fault? I wouldn't risk losing my license or credibility to be a vigilante."

"He's not sure; all he knows is that admin wouldn't risk bad publicity. Also, you're getting a bit of a reputation for being a bad boy these days."

Reeves threw his arms up in the air.

"Please do go on. I'd love to know how I've suddenly become the bad boy of St Lucia," Reeves says with sarcasm.

"Oh, I wasn't talking about your professional actions, mate. I was talking about who you're knocking boots with these days." Justin's grins knowingly.

"You know about Nicole?" Reeves whispers urgently.

"The whole hospital knows, mate. You are aware we have security cameras, yeah?"

Reeves puts his head in his hands.

"Nobody wudda been the wiser if ya hadn't pushed her up against ya car and snogged her. The daft old sod in security room just thought you were giving her a lift home till he saw that. He was a bit surprised you were giving her one, and couldn't keep it to himself." Justin smiles and chuckles to himself.

Reeves looks aggrieved.

"Regretting your decision already?" Justin asked Reeves.

"A little. Nicole, she's just, a little wild..."

Justin nudges Reeves in the shoulder "She knows how you like it, eh Reeves?"

"No, no not like that! She's a little immature and very headstrong. I don't think that anything could happen between us long term."

I walk over to the couch and perch on the suede arm next to Reeves.

"Did Nicole say she wanted something long term?"

"No."

"Then don't worry about it, have some fun with her and let loose..."

"But that's all she ever wants to do. If we're not having sex we're at some bar or club drinking and dancing."

"You're saying this like it's a bad thing."

"Well... no, it's not a bad thing. It's just not my thing; I'd prefer to stay home and watch a movie and relax. My whole day is over-simulating and exhausting. I don't really like having to go out when I have time off."

"Sound like you needs to talk to her about it, but be warned, if you mention it you could very well be going down a relationship avenue. Staying in and cuddling on the couch is relationship territory, and you don't want her getting the wrong idea."

Reeves collapses into the couch putting his hands over his eyes. "Maybe you're right."

Justin smirks "Yeah mate, I'm always right."

Reeves stands and walks over to a cupboard near the lockers, opens it and retrieves a white coat.

"Where are you off too?" Justin asks.

"Back on the floor to maliciously kill more patients," Reeves replies

"Oh don't be like that; you know old Drac is just fooling. I don't think he put much thought into what he said."

"Yeah? Then how did he come to an accusation like that?" Reeves blurts out as he puts on his coat over his pale blue sleeved shirt.

Justin moves uncomfortably "Well he said that you were a chip off the old block."

Reeves stops and turns to Justin.

"You know what they say, the apple doesn't fall far from the tree and such." Justin says quietly.

"I'm not my father."

"No, but there are some similarities. Now that you're dating a nurse it's practically a mirrors image. Although, at least you're not married."

"You've been hanging around Dr Drac for too long, because you're becoming a real dick, Justin." Reeves heads for the door.

"I'm just saying what everyone else is thinking, Reeves!" But Reeves is already out the door and heading along the corridor.

"Asshole!" I yell at Justin, and as I kick at the side table, but instead of my foot going through it I knock it sightly, tipping Justin's drink off the table and onto the floor.

"Shit!" Justin swoops onto the glass then dashes to the sink for a cloth to mop up the spill on the carpet. As I leave the mess to follow after Reeves I hear Justin cursing as he cleans up. I can't help but smile.

CHAPTER 10

I find Reeves on the Emergency floor; he's with a young woman and her baby.

"I just don't know what wrong with him, he's been so fussy and crying a lot and look, there's a rash all over his face, arms and legs." The woman said struggling with a fussy baby on her lap.

"Did he have any kind of fever?" Dr Reeves asks.

"Yeah, that's why I brought him in. The fever got quite high and I was really starting to worry."

"Ok, let's take his temperature and just have a look at his chart then." Reeves', places a thermometer in the child's ear then picks up the child's chart at the end of the bed to note down the result. He thumbs through, looking at observations and nurses notes. Reeves eyebrow cocks at the scrawl written by one of the nurses.

"Jacob isn't vaccinated?"

"No, I don't believe in vaccination," says the mother, struggling to settle her restless child on her lap.

Reeves stares at the mother "You don't believe in vaccination?"

"No, I just think that it's a horrible experience for a baby to suffer upon entering the world, being stuck with needles, which don't really do anything."

"Don't really do anything?" Reeves seems to hang on these words. "You see, I thought your child might have a common childhood sickness because a rash is a common symptom." Reeves begins calmly. "However, because your child hasn't been vaccinated, my possible diagnosis has just increased to several possibilities. He's hot, tired, and probably dehydrated. I'm going to have to run some blood tests to rule out conditions like rubella, measles, chickenpox – all of which can have deadly complications in young children. Since your kid is likely dehydrated, getting blood may take a few goes with a larger, sharper needle than would have been used for a vaccine, and it'll likely take twice as long and several sticks. But we need to find out what he's got because kids used to die from these illnesses before vaccines were invented."

"Jacob is going to die?" the mother squeaked.

"In this instance, I don't think so. It looks like parvovirus to me, not lethal, but we have to check everything, and next time it might be."

"Parvovirus?"

"Slapped-cheek, also known as Fifth's disease. Your kid probably picked it up at day care, where he'll also pick up an array of other diseases, if there's an outbreak." Reeves stands up and leaves the mother open mouthed and staring after him. She clings to her snivelling boy in the sectioned off area for infectious patients.

Margie enters the Emergency floor and Reeves immediately turns his attention to her. He excuses himself from the nurse whom he was briefing on the boy with fever and rash, then walks over to Margie, who is storing away her handbag and coat in the staff area.

"Do you have a moment?" Reeves asks Margie quietly.

Margie smiles and nods politely. Reeves leads her into an empty exam room, locks the door and shuts the blinds.

"Have you got something you want to tell me?"

Margie's face is a complete blank. It's clear she has no idea what he's talking about. "You might have to be more specific?"

"A certain high profile patient was here last week and the lab said that every specimen they received was tampered with. I know I didn't do it."

Margie folds her arms in front of her and looks at Reeves with a stony expression. "I know you didn't, because it was me."

Reeves seems surprised. I doubt he expected a confession so quickly. "You endangered a patient's life intentionally?"

"No, I endangered a child killer's life in the hopes that you couldn't diagnose him."

"Jesus Christ, Margie... what were you thinking?"

Margie stands her ground. She stares at him, but doesn't respond.

"You know your actions fall on my shoulders? It's me who cops the blame!" Reeves hammers his fist on a nearby desk.

Margie seems impassive. "You're young. Barely out of medical school. Your career would have recovered if he'd died."

There's a rap at the door. "Is everything ok in there?" Susie pops her head in.

"Yes!" both Reeves and Margie call back at the same time.

Susie retreats and closes the door.

Reeves lowers his voice to a harsh hiss. "My career might survive, but my reputation wouldn t. Everyone already has a preconception of me and my family. The shit's already flinging in my direction – the rumour mill is in overdrive. I'm going to have to report you. I can't afford to take the blame for this."

Margie's face softens. "Your father was a great doctor, Jason. What happened wasn't his fault. It was just the way people reacted that made it worse, then the gossip blew the whole thing out of proportion. Your father left this hospital because he was grieved, not because he was disgraced."

"I know, but I've seen the way people look at me."

"Nobody here doubts your abilities, Jason, but some who knew your father can see history repeating itself. But this time there's a difference – you don't have a family who are going to be left behind to pick up the pieces and put themselves back together." Margie walks over to the young doctor and puts her hands on his shoulders. Reeves is leaning against the bed his eyes searching the floor.

"I'm sorry, I didn't think about how my actions would affect you." Margie says.

Reeves lifts his head to meet Margie's gaze. "You know I still have to report you. I can't let this come back and fall on me." Reeves says sadly.

"What is there to report? Results have to be redone all the time. The only people who know anything more about it is you, me and Dr Drac. You've diagnosed Barden, treated him, and he's going to trial."

"What about the tests and the rumours of negligence? I don't want people thinking I'm corrupt. You've been with the hospital for decades – nobody ever thinks badly of you. You don't know how it feels. I've only been here six months, and scandal is following me already, even though I haven't done anything."

"The reason I've been here for decades is because I've lived through all the gossip and drama of this hospital. It forges strong connections with other staff that have been here for a long time." Margie puts her arms around Reeves's shoulder in a comforting half hug. "I'll clear things up with Drac and tell him it was me who tampered with the tests."

"You're not worried about Drac's foul temper, or that he'll report you to admin?"

"No, I knew Drac before he was a bitter old man. I use to work with him on the floor before he transferred to the pathology lab."

Reeves laughs "Then do you know Dr Drac's real name?"

Margie stands back and thinks for a moment. "Dancovitch, Dr Levi Dancovitch. He was always a cold, stern man, though. We always kept our heads down and minded our manners when he was doing his rounds..."

I feel a cold shiver down my spine as my mind slips into a memory of a long familiar corridor. I'm carrying starched laundry and can hardly see over the top of the pile when I bump into someone who knocks almost everything to the floor. A tall gawky-looking man with black oiled hair and a large nose picks up his clipboard from the floor, leaving the fallen sheets. He must be in his late twenties, but his haughty expression adds years to his face. He straightens his white coat and barks at me.

"Watch where you're going next time, and keep to one side of the corridor! This is a hospital not a shopping mall." He turns abruptly and heads down the corridor.

I see myself on the floor, picking up the sheets and calling after him in a distressed voice. "I'm sorry sir, I'm sorry!"

While I had experienced flashbacks before, they generally weren't long or vividly detailed. When Margie was describing working with Drac it was like something clicked in my head allowing me to see into the past – my past. It's a new piece in the vast puzzle of my existence. Surely, it couldn't be the same man? Old Drac should have retired years ago – so how do I fit in?

Returning to the present I review my past and am more perplexed than ever.

Margie continues, "...mind you, since we're both still here, Drac has a begrudging respect for me these days".

Reeves nods in response. "So are you going to take care of this? I'm not going to be implicated in any way?"

"No, you're not. I'll sort it with Levi," Margie gives him a reassuring look.

"So we're good? You're not going to try and kill one of my patients again?"

"I was only trying to let nature take its course," Margie says. Reeves looks unimpressed, Margie continues. "Yes, we're good. It was impressive that you could diagnose him without accurate results."

"Drac's assistant, Justin, redrew the blood. But the iron levels were still abnormally high. The damage you did actually helped me diagnose haemochromatosis."

Margie looks disappointed. "Jason, you didn't need to tell me that." Margie bites her lip. "Just like I don't have to tell you that Harold Barden was acquitted of Ben Thompson's murder this afternoon. The forensic evidence that tied Barden to the crime was accidently damaged and the case was dismissed. If you hadn't diagnosed him, if you had let him die, he wouldn't be walking the streets a free man."

"I could have read that in tomorrow's paper and still felt like shit."

"But what the papers wouldn't have mentioned is that there are other victims, not just the Thompson boy. The only difference is that those boys are still alive, but now they have to live the rest of their lives knowing he got away with it again due to insufficient evidence."

With that Margie left Jason Reeves alone in the exam room. He let out an exasperated sigh.

CHAPTER 11

T ING!

I open my eyes, and I'm in Emergency again. The problem with Emergency is it can be hard to figure out who is going to need my help to pass on. I can see Dr Matthews tending to a patient out of the corner of my eye, but I sense her patient isn't the one for me. I glide around the room, not feeling the regular pull of a spirit in need.

I stand off the side and close my eyes, breathe deeply and try to tune in to the familiar sensation. I can feel something, but it's faint. Suddenly the Emergency doors burst open and paramedics hurry towards the operating rooms. Nurse Susie moves beside the cart and trots along with them down towards the operating theatres.

"Here's your stabbing victim. We called ahead for an OR. We can't stop the bleeding"

"OR two is expecting you!" Susie calls after them, then turns back to Emergency.

I hear a faint response of thanks from down the corridor. My body feels pulled towards the victim, and I immediately go into auto response. I sit on the patient's bed and we're wheeled towards the OR. He's a dark-skinned male in his mid-thirties; his breathing is short and quick. He sees me sitting at the bed of the trolley bed.

"Hi," I wave at him, feeling a little awkward. The man licks his thick, parched lips and turns his head away from me.

"I'm not done yet," he manages to squeeze out between gasps.

"If I'm here, it's your time." I reply softly.

"I have a wife and kids. I'm not leaving!" The man looks directly me. "You hear me?! I'm not ready to die!" He says.

My mouth turns into a hard line. It's worse when they fight against me. It feels a bit like I'm killing them, and I don't like it. The paramedic pushing the bed thinks the patient is talking to him, and responds in reassuring tones. "Don't worry; we're going to get you fixed up! We're not going to let you die."

The surgeon is already scrubbed and waiting as our trolley bursts into the OR. The patient is hooked up to machines and the nurse finds a vein on his dark hand and pushes in a sedative. I feel the man's heart slow as if it's my own heart. I know it's time. I rest my hand on his chest and push through to retrieve his soul, but it's still anchored to his body.

The surgeons are moving about me trying to stop the bleeding. "I need three units of O negative in here!" someone calls. I can still hear the bell in my head, and it feels right, it is his time. His blood pressure has dropped, alarms are sounding, and the doctors and nurses are working furiously to locate the bleed. I straddle the body and put another hand into his chest and pull hard.

"Found the bleed! Cauterising."

The man's spirit is slowly coming out of his body; his head is out and his spirit looks older than the body it's occupying. A wrinkled spirit face with bulging eyes screams at me. "Bitch, I told you! I ain't going! Let go!"

I squeal and let go in shock.

"His BP is stabilising. Good job everyone."

The OR is still tense, but there's a collective sigh of relief, a sense that the worst is over. They continue to work on the man, their hands poking through my body as I straddle him. I feel shocked to my core.

"It happens sometimes." I turn to the voice. Niklaus is leaning against the wall. He walks over to me, presents his hand to help me climb down off the bed. "Why don't you ever straddle me like that?"

I'm too shocked to retort to his lewd comment. I accept his hand unthinkingly.

"What just happened?" I ask Niklaus.

"The man's soul is very old. His conscious mind doesn't remember his past lives or that he's died before. But his soul does, and his soul will remain bound to his body for as long as it can."

"Why?" I whisper.

"If you've died before, your spirit becomes more self-aware. When it comes close to the end of its cycle it can hold on tighter to its body in this world if it doesn't want to leave."

"How many times has that soul died?"

Niklaus closes his eyes and breaths deeply. "Sixteen times that I know of, and none have them have been lives lived well."

"Hmm, no wonder he wants to keep a tight hold on this one." I say sadly.

The surgeons are still working on the patient. We stand by the white wall looking on.

"I didn't mean to leave so abruptly the other morning. I was called by the bells." Niklaus says.

I ignore his apology. "Can we get out of here? Out of this room?"

"Sure." Niklaus takes my hand and intertwines his fingers into mine. He walks ahead of me and leads me to the gravel path outside the hospital.

CHAPTER 12

We follow the pathway through the garden towards the old hospital. Niklaus still holds my hand and makes small caressing circles with his thumb. I release his hand and brush a few strands of loose hairs blowing in the wind behind my ear.

"Why are you here tonight?" I ask as I plunge my hands into my pockets

"I sensed that you were in distress and, since that's fairly uncommon in this tiny cage you live in, I thought I'd pop in." Niklaus walks like an old-fashioned gentleman with straight back, squared shoulders and his hands clasped behind him. Sometimes he reminds me of lusty Mr Darcy from *Pride and Prejudice*, but I would never tell him that, of course.

"You can sense me?" I ask, surprised.

"Sometimes."

"Thank you." I turn to him as we walk down the pathway in the darkness. "I'm glad you were here when it happened."

In the corner of my eye I see him shrug. "You're welcome."

We come to a bench and sit. Niklaus stretches his arms out over the bench. There is some distance between us so I don't mind, and there's silence, which is also good.

I take my hands out of my pockets and put them on the wooden bench as I re-adjust my posture and cross one leg over the other. I breathe deep the scent of the night – a faint scent of Jasmine wafts through the veil.

I feel Niklaus's hand on top of mine. I withdraw my hand off the bench and put it on my lap. Niklaus moves closer, closing the gap between us.

"Please?" he asks sweetly.

I look at him he has such sadness in his eyes; it must be hard being continually rejected. I look away from him towards the old hospital. My eye traces the shadow of ivy crawling over the ancient brick facade.

"I have answers," he says. I turn to him and I feel a spark of hope – perhaps this ember could burn through the dark cloud of confusion that is my life?

"I'd be willing to trade..." he says as he slides his hand softly over mine, as it rests in my lap. I don't move.

"Trade what?" I ask, even though I feel I know the answer.

Niklaus moves his head towards my neck and I feel his lips brush my skin. I shrug out of the way. "No!" I stand. "I'm not some common whore, willing to trade sex for secrets!"

"It doesn't have to be sex." Niklaus looks directly at me, and I can sense a mixture of sadness and desperation that almost weakens me. "I just want to be close to you." He says as he stands up straight, putting his hands in his pockets.

Looking down he says, "I'm in love with you."

He looks up at me briefly for a reaction; I feel nothing, and my face probably reveals that emptiness. He is not discouraged.

"I have been since the moment I first saw you. I've loved you through every lifetime you've ever lived."

He reaches out to me and holds my shoulders with both hands as he looks into my eyes, searching for something; maybe a flicker of remembrance?

"Do you know how long it's been? How many lives you've lived while I stand idle on the sideline unable to touch you, unable to kiss you or confess how I feel? I just want to be close to you,

I don't know why I can't move on from you. I feel something for you. I feel as close as I'll ever come to being alive when I'm with you, and I want you to feel something for me. Anything other than malice."

"How can I? I'm confused! I don't know what's real!" I force his hands off my shoulders. "I have fragments of memories that make no sense. But I do remember the first time I met you – that's something I'll never forget!"

I can't remember ever being so exasperated before. I grab my hair at the roots and look at him for some kind of answer. There isn't one, he just stands there. He's not angry or sad he simply looks absent. I emit a growl of agitation then turn my back on him and walk away.

He calls after me. "I can't make you love me, but I can make being closer to me more appealing. Do you really want to be here alone, tortured forever by your existence?"

In spite of myself, I find my feet stopping in their tracks.

"There's information about yourself that you can't remember and I know it bothers you. Inconsistent flickers of memories; some like they were yesterday, and others that are more distant and contradictory. It's obvious you don't love me, so bargaining with you is all I'll ever have."

I turn back around and yell. "This is fucked up; if you made me this way it's your responsibility to tell me who and what I am!"

Niklaus storms towards me and grabs my shoulders again. His face is close to mine and his eyes rage with fury.

"I'm not governed by your way of thinking, nor by your sense of morality! I will do as I please with what I know, and that includes selling it off to you for whatever I see fit." He takes a deep breath and exhales slowly, and then with absolute control he says: "It is only because I respect you that I give you space and abide by your wish that I not be more intimate with you, though it kills me to do so!"

I've never seen Niklaus angry before, and he's gripping my shoulders with such ferocity that it hurts. I wince and gasp in pain. He loosens his grip and whispers, "I could have you if I wanted to. I saved your life, so now it is mine to do with what I want. I'll keep you here for an eternity if I want to."

I stand in shocked silence. My mind is whirling as I try to think of what to do.

Niklaus, seeing my distress, encircles me with his arms. My body is pressed against his; his head against mine. He sighs and I know he's enjoying being close to me, having me submissive in his arms. It baffles me how he can go from barely-controlled fury one moment, to sweet and affectionate in an instant.

With that action I realise he's never going to hate me, never going to leave me. I realise that he truly is in love with me. Though the question is why; it must be something I've forgotten. I decide then and there to push the boundaries further. How far will he let me push his love?

"You respect me?" I shove Niklaus off me. "Should I feel blessed that I've been chosen by you to be stuck somewhere in between life and death? Alone with you? I can't remember the simplest things! Like my name! Do I even have a name? Do you know what it is?"

Niklaus says nothing. He just stands there, giving away nothing.

"Of course you do!" I yell. "You know my name, don't you?"

Niklaus stands with his hands by his sides. He looks smug. Finally, he nods.

"Why won't you tell me? Why don't you tell me anything?!"

Niklaus seems completely detached from emotion. "Everything comes with a cost; it seems you're unwilling to pay at this time."

Niklaus grins a malicious smile. "Sooner or later you will pay it, unable to tolerate not knowing your past."

I blink and he is gone.

CHAPTER 13

I leave the garden and head back to the hospital; dawn is winking over the horizon and I realise I have once again lost time. Another day has begun and I don't recall the time passing. I walk into the doctor's mess and into the on-call room with the heavy blinds covering the windows, and usually a few exhausted occupants within.

Much like showering, I don't need to sleep any more. It's very much a human thing to do, and I suppose that I'm not human anymore. I stretch out onto one of the beds – it's actually clean and freshly made for once. I suppose the cleaners must have been and gone last night. I stare at the ceiling into the darkness and churn over what Niklaus has said to me. Suppose he does have some answers – am I prepared to prostitute myself for them? If I am, how far would I let his hands explore me, and what acts would he want me to provide for his entertainment. Could I ever have sex with Niklaus?

A small flicker of a memory inflicts my mind. I'm naked and wrapped against Niklaus's sheet-clad body. Is it a memory? Or my imagination? A smile, a whisper, a kiss and it's gone.

I ask myself if I am I willing to sleep with Niklaus. Perhaps I already have? Memory beguiles me. I roll onto my side and through the darkness is a sleeping Reeves, his breathing is so deep and slow that I didn't even realise he was here. The beds are squeezed close together, designed to provide as many doctors as possible with the opportunity to rest when exhaustion takes over.

All of the faint lines that usually show Reeves' concerned, stressed or exhausted expressions have all faded into nothingness, leaving only a relaxed peaceful expression in its place. Reeves seems younger now than I've ever seen him. I realise he is in fact a handsome man, with his straight nose, full lips, chiselled jaw and smooth skin, although he does look a little pale. Somehow his light hair matches his pale complexion and suggests angelic features. I haul myself up and lean over his peaceful face. Yes, I can see why Nicole flatters him and takes every opportunity to be close to him.

I find myself wondering if Reeves was popular at school. I decide not; he's a reserved, shy, intelligent man, not the usual criteria for teenage popularity among peers. The older nurses say he looks like his father, and they're right. I remember Elwood Reeves quite well – he was tall, handsome and had a bravado that he coasted on; quick with a joke or a sidelong leer at the young nurses on shift. His son doesn't have these qualities, although he's smart like his father. His lack of self-confidence is probably a combination of living in his father's shadow, as well as the limitations of his recent graduation from medical school.

Warm feelings return to me when I think of Reeves Senior, and I wonder if we could have ever been close if we'd been in the real world together. I did harbour a crush on him for many years, and I was grateful to be invisible to him so that he couldn't see me blush when I watched him work. I convinced myself that he would look in my direction sometimes, as if he knew I was there.

I sink to my knees and can feel Reeves Junior's breath on my face through his slightly parted lips. I can see he's taken the trouble to shave before crashing into bed to sleep for a few hours, and I can't resist running my fingers along the smoothness of his cheek. He groans a little and rolls onto his back, leaving enough room for me to perch on the edge of his bed. I lean over him and watch his chest rise and fall in slumber. Consumed with longing to be close to someone other than Niklaus I lean over and brush his lips against mine. It's not the same as being kissed by Niklaus; with him I can actually feel his lips against mine, but with Reeves I just feel the lightest flutter of a butterfly's wing, causing a tiny zing on my lips, like an electric spark that reverberates to my core.

Suddenly, I have a flash of Elwood Reeves, locking lips with me passionately in a similar room. It must have been many years ago – the old hospital! I struggle to cast my mind back through the mists of time. Panting to taste Elwood's lips again... feeling his erect member pressing into my thigh through my starched uniform.

"Wait, not here," Elwood whispers urgently.

"Why not? Nobody will miss us if we're quick," I breathe back.

Elwood locks the door and turns back to me, with one quick swoop he hoists up my skirts and is unclasping my suspender clips.

Though I desperately try to cling to the vision, it fades to nothing, but I've worked out what happened. I realise I've had an affair with a married man, and this memory was sparked because I was kissing his son! How many other memories are locked away in my mind, waiting for the right trigger to set them free? Maybe I don't need Niklaus as much as he thinks I do? Although, it could take an eternity trying to fill in the gaps on my own, and it seems my morals have been questionable in the past. Perhaps I could give a little more to Niklaus to gain a little more insight into who I was before I came to this place? With much to consider, I leave the room and soon find myself drifting after a nurse on her rounds.

CHAPTER 14

Reeves, having awoken from his sleep in the on-call room, rises and sits on the edge of the bed. He yawns and rubs his eyes before fumbling for his shoes under the bed. After slipping the comfortable loafers on he goes through into the main room, making a beeline straight for the coffee machine, which someone considerate must have freshly brewed. He pours himself a cup and blows lightly on the hot elixir of wakefulness before tentatively sipping the contents. Peering up at the clock he calculates he has ten minutes left before he is needed on the floor, so he pulls a chair out from under the table and picks up yesterday's newspaper.

CASE DISMISSED FOR CHILD MURDERER

Reeves lets out a deep sigh while skimming over the article's contents, feeling the weight of a heavy stone in his belly. Margie was right to say it might have been better if the man had died; though this contradicted with his morals and the code of ethics that had been instilled in him throughout medical school. His eyes follow the printed words without any of the meaning absorbing. His mind drifts away and is filled with imagined images of the family's reaction to the news that the man who killed their son has been set free on a technicality. And from what Margie insinuated, this wasn't the only boy who had been traumatised by this monster. Dr Reeves swallowed hot coffee that burnt his mouth; but he felt he deserved more punishment than that for curing the man who brutally beat and molested a child then dumped his body near an overpass. He couldn't help wonder if management allocated him this case because he was fresh from medical school – unlikely to properly diagnose the mysterious illness and hope the patient doesn't survive. Troubled with guilt, Reeves places his mug into the sink and walks out onto the floor. He finds Nicole and asks if she wants to go out tonight. He hides his lack of enthusiasm for her company, because he knows Nicole is wild and likely to distract from the internal conflict that rages within him. Nicole beams delightedly and accepts his invitation.

CHAPTER 15

I t seems like I've been mulling over Niklaus's proposal for days, although I really don't know what days are any more – it could easily have been months. But I've come to the conclusion that I'm going to have to be more agreeable to him if I want to find my way out of here, or at least find out where here is.

I recall the flicker of another memory about Dr Reeves Senior from the on-call room: My hair released from the restraints of my nurse's cap and flowing down my naked back... Dr Elwood Reeves below me, his tanned skin showing through his open shirt... me kissing him deeply to stifle his moans while I grind in rhythm with him. Yes I could do it; I could bend a man to my will – perhaps I still can. And maybe this time I can get what I want without compromising myself too much?

I wander up to geriatrics and linger in the darkness of the unlit waiting room. Only the security lights outside give the room a soft haze.

Perhaps he will come if I call? "Niklaus?" I feel like a fool, calling his name.

"Niklaus, where are you?" I look around and still nothing.

"Niklaus, please! I've considered your offer!" I turn around and he's standing there in the doorway.

I walk up to him and put my hands on his shoulders running them down his arms "Oh Niklaus..." I sigh longingly just as Nicole did. "I'm so glad to see you..." I press my body against his but cannot bring myself to hold his hands, so I hold his wrists instead. His body is tense.

"You're glad to see me?" Niklaus seems suspicious and he doesn't respond to my body against his.

"Yeah, I've considered what you said. I think you're right. We only have each other in this existence and I should feel blessed that I've been chosen by you."

"That isn't what you said last time we met. You told me it was unfair that I would hide things from you after putting you in this state."

I put my finger to his lips to hush him. "I'm sorry, I was wrong. I'm ok with the terms so long as they're fair. I do enjoy your touch – it's nice to be reminded I'm not alone..."

Not entirely false; it is nice on the odd occasion to have Niklaus near. I look up into his eyes for an answer. He's searching mine and I sense he wants to believe me, but after our last conversation I don't blame him if he's uncertain.

Niklaus lifts his hands and cups my cheeks. I know from that look he wants to lean in to kiss me. "Wait." I whisper urgently. "What do I get in return?"

Niklaus closes his eyes for a moment and sighs. When he opens them he seems more assured. "A question answered."

"Just one?"

"One question that befits the action."

"Then this is too much!" I pull his hands off my cheeks. "I know how much a kiss from me would mean to you. I'll save it until later."

I can see the hurt in Niklaus's eyes, oh so briefly before it's replaced with cunning. "What's your question?"

"Who am I?"

Niklaus chuckles and shakes his head "No, that question would deserve at least a kiss. Think again."

I take a moment to think. "What am I?"

Niklaus gestures for me to sit at the end of a rectangular bench seat in the centre of the room. Held by my word I do as I'm told. I sit on the edge of the cushioned bench facing away from him, but now I'm feeling nervous. I want my voice to sound authoritative, but when I speak it tremors. "When I say stop, it means I think your question has been paid. Understand?" How does Nicole make this look easy?

"Take off your jacket." Niklaus says.

Still sitting, I slowly unbutton my jacket and feel it slide it off my shoulders and slither to the floor. I wait silently in my black tank top and jeans when I hear something drop on the floor and I look behind me to see Niklaus's dark grey trench coat lying in a crushed puddle beside mine. I look ahead again and I sense him straddling the bench... then his hands are on my skin, my arms and shoulders. I close my eyes and a small shiver goes down my spine as I feel his skin against my own. I hear him sigh with longing as he brings himself closer to me and I can feel a bulge pressing against the base of my spine.

He pulls back my hair off my neck and whispers in my ear.

"You're like me. You are Death..."

Niklaus runs his hands up my arms and hooks his fingers under the slim strap of my top, easing them off my shoulders.

"Except you seem drawn only to those who need you, spirits that are having difficulty crossing over."

"Why?" I ask.

"Can I kiss your neck?" Niklaus asks tentatively. "I want to feel your skin against my lips..."

"Not yet." I say with more assertiveness than I feel.

Niklaus sighs and pushes the straps of my top back onto my shoulders. He wraps an arm around my waist and I feel his hand moving over my clothed legs.

"Why am I stuck in this hospital?"

His hand moves into my inner thigh...

"Because you died here..."

His hand is inching up higher, I grip his hand stopping it in its place at the top of my inner thigh.

"When?"

"Over forty years ago now."

"How?"

Niklaus laughs in the back of his throat "I'm going to need more if you want more answers."

I think of what I'm willing to sacrifice, "You can kiss my neck." I say point-blank.

Niklaus can sense that I really want to know this answer. "Will you face me?" he says as he moves his hand from my inner thigh and pulls back a few stray strands of hair off my neck.

"No. But you can kiss my neck and my shoulders." I lean my body into him and relax my head on his shoulder exposing my neck to him. Lifting my head I whisper in his ear.

"This is what you wanted wasn't it? To be able to feel my skin against your lips."

This is my sincerest attempt at enticing Niklaus, and I can sense him weakening.

"Perhaps next time I'll wear something more revealing for you," I whisper.

His breathing has slowed and it's heavier. As a final push I rub my hand against his thigh down to his knee over his dark slacks.

Niklaus lets out a resigned sigh.

"You were shot."

"By whom?" I still have my hand firmly on his leg.

"A patient." Niklaus claims his reward and kisses my neck tenderly at first, and then his kisses increase in ferocity. I shrug away from his lips.

"What else? What happened?" I ask.

Niklaus can't talk while he's devouring my neck. I hear him

groan slightly and I can feel him grinding against my back. I grab his other knee and push myself up, slightly out of his reach.

"What else?" I demand.

Niklaus groans in agony.

"Please Ava, please... I want more of you!"

My body stiffens and my eyes widen as I swing round to face him.

"Ava? Is that my name?"

Niklaus loosens his grip on me, then rests his forehead on my shoulder and sighs. After a moment of thought Niklaus lifts his head and removes his hands from me.

"Deciding what you're going to trade for a simple yes or no answer?" I ask.

"Yes." Niklaus gets up off the chair and picks up his coat and puts it on.

I turn to him. "Yes what? Is Ava my name? Where are you going?"

"I've lost my interest in this game for now, but I have no doubt I'll be seeing you soon."

Niklaus crouches down to my height and pecks me on the cheek. "Goodnight Ava."

Without warning he vanishes in front of me and I'm left looking around at the gloomy waiting room of the geriatric ward.

Ava. At least I have a name now.

CHAPTER 16

It's a quiet night in the Emergency room, although I know none of the nurses will say the 'Q' word, as it appears health staff are still superstitious, even in these modern times. I'm wearing a stolen cocktail dress with a wide tulle skirt that swishes as I flounce my hips from side to side and swirl around the room, weaving between beds and oblivious patients.

The red phone's distinctive chime halts me mid-swirl. Margie plucks it up and starts to scribble down notes. She stops mid-sentence and draws a sharp breath, puts down the pen and holds the phone with both hands, her mouth drops open and she begins hurriedly speaking into the phone. Two vertical creases form between her eyebrows. I swipe my coat from the back of a chair and move to the nurses' station. Matthews, catching the expression on Margie's face, leans in with interest. Margie holds her hand over the receiver and whispers urgently.

"The paramedics are bringing in a young male who collapsed at a club. They couldn't find ID but one of the paramedics says he looks like Jason Reeves."

Matthews' expression doesn't change upon hearing this news; she just gives a slight nod and goes outside the building to meet the ambulance and gets there as it screeches to a stop. The back doors fly open and Matthews climbs into the vehicle, startling the paramedic within. She inspects the young man on the trolley then barks at the paramedic.

"What happened?"

"Onlookers say he just collapsed. Nobody seemed to know much of anything," the burly man replies.

"Was he with anyone?" Matthews asks.

"Not that we could see. It's that doctor – Reeves, isn't it?" the paramedic says with concern in his voice.

Matthews' eyes are directed to the burly man quizzically.

"It's not often a doctor comes out to greet us personally," the paramedic admits.

Matthews looks back down to the unconscious man and then back to the paramedic.

Matthews puts an oxygen mask over the man's face.

"Take this man directly though Emergency into one of the vacant side rooms. I'll meet you in there." She pulls the thin blanket over the man's face. Matthews exits the vehicle and strides down the corridor in pursuit of the burly paramedic and his partner. I have to run to keep up with them.

"Margie!" Matthews barks across the room. "Call upstairs to maternity or paediatrics and tell them we need a doctor down here ASAP to cover me." Matthews commands.

"Is it?" Margie asks holding the phone receiver in hand tightly.

"Yeah, it is." Matthews replies coolly.

Matthews enters the examination room and moves to the patient.

"Reeves, can you hear me? It's Matthews, you're at St Lucia." Reeves tosses and mutters incoherently. "Has he been conscious during the ride over?" Matthews asks the paramedic who is loitering near the door.

"Sort of, he's been in and out... His BP has been really high the whole time."

Matthews nods "You can go."

As the paramedics leave, I drift over and take a close look at the patient. His breathing is laboured and his skin is covered with a film of sweat. It is Jason Reeves.

Matthews flashes a torch in Jason's eyes to check his pupils, but before she can assess his condition he begins convulsing.

"Margie, get in here!" Matthews holds him down so he can't hurt himself. Even though I haven't heard the familiar TING, I know it's coming. I sit at the end of the bed, and wait with a heaviness inside.

Margie bursts into the room and is immediately at Jason's side assisting Matthews. I hear the TING. He stops seizing and both women relax momentarily before alarms begin to go off for his vitals; the TING is getting louder in my head. I ignore it.

"BP is spiking; he's going into cardiac arrest!" Matthews says as Margie races across the room for a crash cart.

The TING becomes louder, this time ringing in my ears; I pull my knees up to my chest and put my hands over my ears as a tear slides down my cheek.

Matthews has one knee on the bed and has begun compressions. Margie preps the paddles of the defibrillator.

TING!

I don't want to be the one who kills Reeves.

TING!

This noise is screaming at me! My head hurts! I shake my head back and forth holding my head in my hands.

"Not me, not me! Please! I don't want to be the one who kills Reeves! Please!" I beg aloud to the ceiling, but I know no one can hear.

Jason's spirit is fighting for release from its earthly body. It looks like agony. Choking back tears I reach out and clasp his spirit; it flows with ease into my hand.

"I'm sorry Jason, I'm so sorry..." I hold his spirit to my body and he feels real, I can touch him; feeling the fabric of his shirt against my cheek, staining it in tears. "I didn't want to be the one, please know this!" I look up into his face and he looks shocked, surprised even; he does not push me off as I had expected, but he does not comfort me either.

"Where am I?" he asks simply, looking down into my eyes.

"In between..." that's all I can bring myself to say.

"What?" Reeves says still dazed.

From the corner of my eye I can see the after-light forming. I know that once he sees it he'll forget his life and lose the fight. I look to Matthews and Margie who are still madly trying to save his life. They just need more time...

I kneel in front of Reeves and hold his face and say, "Jason, whatever happens don't stop looking at me. Your life depends upon it. Don't be tempted to turn around. Whatever you hear, ignore it!"

His eyes widen. "Why? What's behind me?"

I caress his cheek with my thumb. "Because you are looking directly at Death and behind you is the afterlife. As soon as you see it you won't be able to come back and you have more you need to do in this lifetime. You don't deserve to die; I want you to live." I had never meant anything more in my life; I want him to live with every fibre of my body and soul.

"Who are you? Why do you get to decide?"

"I don't get to decide, but I'm going to try and give you time. All anyone ever wants is more time and that's what I want to give to you, Jason." My voice falters and a sob escapes my throat. I can't speak but I can't stop holding his face in my hands. I don't understand why, after hundreds of lives have slipped through my fingers to the other side... why should this be any different?

Jason puts his hands onto my shoulders, and I feel the warm embrace of a comforting hug. Over his shoulder I can see a woman dressed in a cream fitted suit; her face is stern and she is glaring at me.

I lean up and whisper in Jason's ear.

"Whatever happens, remember what I said. It's a trick. Don't listen to anything you hear from behind you, and don't give in to the desire to turn away from me. Just focus on me, my voice... and don't let go."

Jason nods and puts his hands around my waist, holding me tight, and I rest my hands on his shoulders. It's like a slow dance between lovers, but it's a life and death dance between strangers. I pull him close and keep his eyes locked on mine.

"Who are you?"

"Ava. My name is Ava."

"How do you know my name?"

"I know almost everything about you. I've been watching you."

Jason cocks his head to one side and looks like a curious puppy.

"Like a guardian angel?"

"Let go of him! Let go of my son, you whore! I let you have my husband, but you will not have my son!"

With my eyes wide with shock, I turn to the woman who is addressing me.

"I'm sorry, I don't know who you are..."

"Mum?" Jason begins to turn his head.

"Jason, no!" I scream as I turn his head back towards me then crush his lips with mine in a passionate exchange. My mind is flooded with memories of being intimate with Elwood Reeves. Memories I thought were lost seem to unlock when I'm close to Jason, and with it a deep feeling that can only be described as a primal lust between us. Sparks fly as we kiss and the electricity goes down my spine to my core.

Our kiss breaks and I gasp for breath, my eyes wide in the shock of recognition. Reeves is still dazed; he must have felt something too, but perhaps not to the same degree as me. In an attempt to recapture more of my memories, I kiss Reeves again and pull him closer still, I feel a tingle down my spine and the pounding of his heart against my chest. Jason's hands are moving from my waist to my back, one tangles in my hair, pulling a little which makes me groan out loud. Our lips part once more just as his spirit fades like smoke through my fingertips as he returns back to his body.

I hear the woman's voice behind me shriek, and the word 'whore' echoes around me before her presence implodes into light and she vanishes.

My attention is diverted to Jason's body as he gasps for a deep breath of air. Margie falls onto his chest with tears of joy in her eyes, a hand caressing his semi-conscious face.

Jason's eyes flicker at the warmth on his cheek and he utters softly. "Mum?"

I smile to myself, delighted to have found a way to recover a flash of a memory I thought I had lost, as well as the remembrance of my sensuality and sexual agency. I hadn't realised I'd missed that sense of power and invincibility; like the world would bow down at my feet with a sweet word and a bat of my eyelash. I know now that I was good at it, making Elwood sigh, moan and he would bend to my will in any way I asked of him.

Another piece of the puzzle has fallen in place and I feel renewed.

I look around and see Niklaus standing off to the side in a darkened corner of the room. His arms are crossed, his jaw is set hard and his eyes are dark, cold and hard. Holding my gaze he drops his arms to his side and walks to me, as I'm kneeling on Jason's bed like a watchful guardian.

I sense an impending rebuke but I'm still drunk with a sense of power and exhilaration.

"Niklaus... Did you enjoy watching the show?"

Niklaus breaks his gaze from me and looks down at Jason. He raises his hand and hovers it over Jason's unconscious body.

"Don't!"

I grab Niklaus's wrist, but he doesn't move his hand. My grip is firmly around his wrist and we are locked in a battle of wills.

He hisses into my face. "You shouldn't have done that. His soul will have a deep gash in it now."

"I don't care! I wanted him to live."

With all my strength I push against Niklaus's hand and he stumbles backwards away from the bed. His usual stony expression is gone and he looks shocked and hurt, and I'm surprised to see, almost human. He drops his hand to his side and looks down.

I'm aware that Margie and Matthews are buzzing around Jason, stabilising his condition and running assessments, but on our plane it's like we're in a void where time is sucked in and holds us captive.

"Why can't you kiss me like that?" he asks quietly.

"But, I do," I purr, the remnants of my new found confidence still lingering.

"No, when you kiss me you're going through the motions. When you kissed him just now you were passionate and wanting..."

"...wanting to keep him alive. That's all," I insist.

There's the briefest moment of silence while Niklaus contemplates my words.

"Ava, I want you to kiss me like that, and not for any reward or information, but because you want to."

Like a small flicker of a flame igniting into a blaze an idea occurs to me.

I climb off the bed toward Niklaus and I look him deeply in the eyes.

"Is that all you want from me, Niklaus? For me to kiss you like that?"

He rests his hands on my shoulders.

"I want you to love me, Ava."

"Love?"

I had only ever thought of his affection as obsession, never anything deeper, but the torment in his eyes convinces me he's genuine. His voice softens and he continues.

"I've loved you so deeply and for so long that I feel like I'm chasing..."

I lean up and kiss Niklaus to stop him saying any more. I press my body into his and I linger on his lips and feel his arms wrap around me as the kiss deepens and I feel a flutter of a distant memory; a smile followed by a giggle and the smell of a familiar perfume lingers in my nostrils. I kiss Niklaus again and tangle my fingers in his hair and deepen the kiss, feeling, wanting, like never before. I break the kiss but keep my close proximity and look into Niklaus's eyes.

"Is that what you wanted, Niklaus? Was that enough passion and wanting?"

Niklaus doesn't reply. I peck him quickly on the lips teasingly and let go of him.

I remove my coat, exposing the black sweetheart dress underneath. With a sly smile I walk away from Jason now that I sense he's going to be alright, and I'm certain Niklaus will dare not touch him for fear I will lose my sudden playful attitude. I move to the door and wander into the empty exam room just off the main Emergency room, looking over my shoulder to make sure Niklaus is following. He is, and he seems intrigued.

Inside the empty, dark room I pull myself up onto the bed and spread my legs, wordlessly inviting Niklaus to stand between my thighs. I pull him close to me and kiss him again. Niklaus breaks the kiss this time, but keeps his face close to mine, his voice husky with desire, but his eyes sharp with suspicion.

"What's the matter with you? I haven't seen you like this..."

I pout like a sullen child and chastise him with a mocking tone.

"Oh, Niklaus, all your dreams are coming true and you're analysing the situation. Why?"

His mouth twitches in amusement, and his eyes soften as he kisses me again. It looks like he's setting aside his reservations to indulge in his desires. I don't resist and I don't push him away. This is what I want. I want him to lose himself, be vulnerable and then I can leave him wanting more.

I push off his heavy black coat and it falls to the floor. His hands move under my dress and up my outer thighs, pulling me closer to him. I let out a small noise of surprise and Niklaus stops abruptly, his body stiffens but his hands stay firmly in place. I smile then realise he probably can't see me in the dark so I lean up and kiss him lightly and I feel his body relax. I wrap my arms around his neck and pull him closer and kiss him deeply. He reciprocates and my hands move from his neck to his button up shirt. I fumble around the hand-sewn button hole and squeeze a mother-of-pearl button through the hole. Niklaus stops kissing me but his mouth lingers near mine. My fingers find the second button and push it free from its hold, as I kiss the corner of his lips. He still doesn't move nor speak, so I unbutton a third smooth shell disk and push the material aside so I can kiss his smooth, lean chest. My lips move closer to the nape of his neck and I kiss him lightly again and again as I undo the rest of his buttons. I breathe the scent of his flesh as I run my hands over his smooth, toned and surprisingly beautiful torso. I am reminded of the marbled perfection chiselled by ancient craftsmen.

I look up at him and see a face awash with contentment. He pushes my hair back off my shoulder and runs his hand down the back of my arm, then kisses me tenderly and smiles.

This is a side of Niklaus I've never seen. The way he is behaving is almost mortal; he's living within the moment with me. The way he is so at ease and gentle makes me curious.

"What are you thinking about, Niklaus?" I whisper softly, hoping not to break the spell.

Niklaus strokes my cheek and kisses my forehead before he answers. "I just want this to be real, but experience tells me it's not..."

"Then why are you smiling?"

After a moment of silence Niklaus replies. "I just want to enjoy this moment, even if I'm being played."

"I remembered a part of me..."

Niklaus eyes open wide. "Really?" he draws a sharp breath. "Do you remember us?"

"Us?" The urgent pleading of his eyes makes me want to say yes, in spite of my new sense of power, but I can't bring myself to lie to him.

"No, not really, but I feel it sometimes, I can feel a memory, buried deep, of being with you. I know you like certain things... like when I kiss you here."

I kiss the nape of his neck and he swallows hard to stifle a moan. I smile a little and feel so powerful. I grab hold of Niklaus's hips and pull him closer to me so our groins are touching through clothing. I whisper in his ear,

"I remember how good it feels to have someone between my legs..."

I suckle at his earlobe and I can feel his cock twitch, this time he gives in and lets me hear him moan while his hands move up and cup my breasts over my clothing. I put my hand firmly over his and halt its progress. Niklaus looks at me with an ironic smile.

"What do you want? What do you want in exchange for this?"

"Nothing," I mutter.

"With you and me, it's always been an exchange. I can't think of any reason why you would suddenly change your approach, so I assume you want something."

He's right, of course. He knows me well. I'd better make the most of this moment and choose my question well.

"How do I pass on from here?"

Niklaus lets go of me and stands for a moment before replying.

"I don't think you can. You're stuck here."

Stuck here. Here. On this plane that doesn't even have a name.

I feel a crushing weight in my chest, a weight that is spreading to the rest of my body and smothering my sensual energy. I had always hoped Niklaus would know of some method for my release; some ritual or spell that would undo the endless nightmare that is my existence. But now I have the answer to my question, and somehow I know that Niklaus is telling me the truth.

Throughout my time confined within these hospital walls, I've often hovered on the edge of insanity, trying to make sense of my existence while carrying out the unsung duties of Death. Once, after endless weeks of coaxing confused souls out of their earthly bodies and seeing them safely into the next plane, I found myself functioning beyond exhaustion, feeling isolated and drained. *Enough. No more. I can't do this anymore.* Words like a mantra repeating in my head as I moved to the rooftop, as if in a trance. When I walked through the rooftop door and felt a waft of warm air in my face, the ledge beckoned me like an oasis in the desert. I didn't have second thoughts, there was no need; I knew what I had to do. I had already decided before I made the journey to the roof. I knew I'd had done my best and I had nothing left to give. I didn't hover on the edge of the building and contemplate my existence. I stretched my arms wide as if on the top of a diving board, took a deep breath, feeling nothing but relief and exhilaration, then stepped over the edge. Gravity didn't plunge me downwards as I expected. Instead I wafted down like a feather caught in a breeze. I craved the resounding thud of my body hitting pavement, but instead when I eventually landed face down and splayed out. I barely felt the impact, and was, unfortunately, completely unharmed.

Disappointed, but still determined, I hauled myself up and wandered into the hospital. A tray of utensils were waiting to go into the autoclave. I eyed a scalpel and its sharp blade begged me to pick it up, but already doubt was nagging at me. I thought it wouldn't work, but I had to be sure. I pushed through the veil and clutched the instrument. Running the blade length-way down my wrists I managed to make a cut into the flesh, but no blood poured forth. I inspected the wound and could see the tendons beneath like a cross-sectioned cadaver. By the time I put the scalpel down on the counter and looked back at my arm, the deep gash had already sealed up, leaving no mark. Death wouldn't be a means of escape, and the afterlife portals had rejected me, so I had pinned all my hopes on Niklaus. And now, with the words, 'You're stuck here', that option is closed to me as well. I should feel devastated, but instead I feel detached.

Niklaus leans in to kiss me, no doubt eager to claim his reward. I can think of no reason to object, so I angle my chin up towards him. Suddenly, he stops, and though still staring into my eyes, he pulls away from me. My eyebrows pucker in confusion as I analyse the situation and what has just passed between us. I can see no reason for his hesitation. Niklaus casts his eyes down and seems to be deep in thought. Releasing my shoulders, he steps further away from me. My heart flutters with fear and confusion – this is everything he's ever wanted, yet he looks conflicted. He picks up his coat from the floor and shrugs into it.

"Where are you going?"

"I'll be around. I just need to be away from you for now."

"What happened?"

"Nothing."

"I thought this is what you wanted"

"I thought it was too. In a way it is, but…" Niklaus pauses, he looks off into the distance then down at his shoes. His shirt is still open, contrasting the black of his shirt and dark heavy overcoat against the white of his skin. I look over his exposed figure, every muscle toned, and immoral skin that will never age or blemish. Something deep within me rises to the surface and a foreign feeling takes root. I don't want Niklaus to go, I want his hands on me again. I snap myself out of my thoughts and seek a logical conclusion. *That can't be right. Perhaps I just don't want to be rejected.* I meet Niklaus's eye line as he offers a hesitant explanation.

"…it's not as satisfying as I thought it would be. This experience… it's just not real."

With my newfound sensual persona, I thought I could win him over. I thought I had found the answer key to the Niklaus test and that all of my desires could be fulfilled with this new sense of self. Apparently I was wrong. Niklaus had sensed the hollowness of my actions and rebuked my advances. He looks as though he's about to leave but I want to try and salvage this interaction.

"Niklaus?"

Niklaus lifts his head and looks to me silently. I wonder if he'll tell me something I've often wondered and never felt ready to ask until now.

"Niklaus, I know that you love me. But did I love you?"

"Yes. From the moment you first saw me." He leans in and kisses me on the cheek. "But that was a very, very long time ago." I hoped evoking those old memories might entice him back, instead, he vanishes before my eyes.

My mind is whirling around reliving the conversation and its implications for my time here. I need to shut it out but there's no escape in sleep. The gurney I'm sitting on has a thin mattress and pillow in this empty exam room and I draw my knees up to my chest, roll on to my side and curl up into the foetal position. At least I can close my eyes and try to zone out for a while.

I begin to process my day and its events. My eyes flick open. I bolt upright as if waking from a nightmare. "Reeves!"

CHAPTER 17

It took me a while to track Jason down. I couldn't see his name on any patient lists on any of the wards, so the hospital must have listed him and his details as confidential, probably trying to limit the spread of gossip that would already be flooding the hospital. That meant I had to wander into every room in the hospital before I finally found him in a small private room at the end of a corridor. When I arrived Reeves was still unconscious, and Matthews was standing at the end of his bed reviewing his chart.

I'm happy to hang here watching him. It's not like I've got anything better to do, and I feel a little responsible for bringing him back when Niklaus clearly doesn't want him here. Part of me is also hopeful that being close to Jason might trigger more lost memories from my past.

Jason begins to rouse, and a spasm of pain flinches across his features as he tries to shift his limbs into a more comfortable position. His bloodshot eyes scan the room and he groans as he shifts his neck towards Dr Matthews. She moves to the seat beside the bed, clipboard in hand, and she begins to scribble some notes as Jason adapts to his surroundings.

"Evening Jason," Matthews says, without looking up from her clipboard.

"Is it still evening?"

"Sunday evening. You've been asleep all day."

Jason emits a soft groan.

Matthews continues. "How are you feeling?"

Jason leans back into the pillow, eyes shift to the ceiling and he seems to be assessing himself.

"Not great. My body is aching and my head thumping," he says while reaching his hand to his face and pressing the indentations on the ridge of his eyebrows.

Matthews reaches for a remote and presses the button then continues with her paperwork.

As the pain medication hit his veins, his hand drops from his face, and the tension eases from his face.

"Thank you."

She nods.

"What are you writing?" Jason asks.

"An incident report"

Jason's complexion goes white and his eye widen slightly. It seems the gravity of the situation he's in has just hit him.

"I need to know what you took last night, Jason."

Jason looks surprised. "You didn't do a tox screen?"

"No. That's why I need to know what you took." Matthews is blunt with her words and it's hard for me to tell what she's thinking. She brushes back a few loose strands of hair that had fallen in front of her face and looks at Jason for a response.

"Wellbutrin. I'm trying to quit smoking – I must have accidently taken it twice."

I believe him so I'm not sure why Matthews looks sceptical. Her face is a blank slate, and she gives nothing away on how she is going to deal with this situation.

Maybe she's remembering that doctor who was dismissed in disgrace a few years ago. Davies, I think his name was. He was caught smoking marijuana with the orderlies after his shift. Matthews never had much time for him because he wore his hair long in a ponytail – she used to call him the hippy – but I recall she was upset about him losing his job.

Matthews holds the power to make Reeves's life miserably tedious with mandatory drug testing and counselling. And she'll take a risk with her own career if she covers up his actions. I hope my intervention doesn't cause Jason a world of financial and legal hurt.

"What's going on with you, Reeves?" Matthews asks.

Jason looks away from Matthews, he seems to have fixed his eye on the far wall.

"Nothing. I'm fine. I told you, I accidentally took my meds twice."

Matthews sighs as she puts the clipboard down on the bed.

"Jason, you're one of the most dedicated doctors I've worked with in a long time. You're doing well for someone so young..."

Jason's eyebrows peak in surprise. I'd never heard Matthews give a compliment and I don't think Jason had either. It isn't that Matthews is unkind; she just generally keeps her opinions of others to herself.

"...but you're too emotional."

Jason looks almost offended.

"You take everything to heart and I think it's dragging you down. You'll need to learn to compartmentalise if you want to be a better doctor. I need you to be logical, methodical and above all I need you to be mentally and physically sound."

"I'm fine! I'm just a little overworked and was trying to blow off some steam."

"I don't think you're understanding the gravity of this situation. You were found unconscious on a dance floor at three in the morning. It's almost impossible to cover up this type of behaviour. I don't have the time or the patience to tend to your patients while you're attending mandatory counselling sessions and jumping through administration hoops to satisfy them that you're not a liability."

"Give me a break, Matthews! It was just a night out that went a bit wrong."

"A bit wrong? It seems to me you work yourself nearly to death, then on your time off you take too many pills and drink yourself nearly to destruction with that nurse! What are you trying to do? Kill yourself?"

Reeves looks aghast. "I didn't try to commit suicide if that's what you're thinking!"

"It looks to me like you're in a tail-spin– so maybe you didn't intentionally try to commit suicide, but even a first year medical student knows that alcohol increases the effects of some medications..." Matthews puts quote marks around the word 'medications' with her fingers as she speaks. "...and the effects can be fatal."

"But I'm fine!"

"You died."

The colour drains from Jason's already pale face, and the look of shock tells me he doesn't remember anything from our encounter.

Matthews waits a beat to let the information sink in before continuing.

"You were dead for two minutes."

"What happened?"

"You went into cardiac arrest and then everything stopped. We tried to revive you, but after a while, I gave up." Matthews looks down at her hands and I see the first emotion I've ever seen cross her face – guilt. Her voice softens.

"Jason, I need to know whether this was an accident, or whether it was..."

Jason stares straight ahead and his words are spoken firmly through a clenched jaw. "It was an accident. I double-dosed Wellbutrin and I drank more than I realised while I was out."

Matthews scrutinises Jason's face and spends a few moments in deliberation.

"Ok. You smoke don't you, Reeves?"

Jason nods in answer.

"Good."

Jason's eyes flick up to Matthews who begins to scribble away on the clipboard again. When the scribbling stops she stands up straight and her persona is back to that of the efficient, cool professional.

"Wellbutrin is used as a cease smoking aid, but has also been known to induce seizures in high doses. It's an unfortunate chain of events that you *accidently* double-dosed then decided to go to a dance club which had strobe lights. Perhaps in future you could be a little more careful Dr Reeves?"

Matthews passes two forms to Jason, I come closer to the bed to see what she's given him.

"Just in case you forget what happened." she says.

I look down at the paperwork. It's her incident report and one blank incident form for Reeves to fill out.

Jason nods again and thanks her as she turns to leave the room.

As Matthews reaches the door, Jason calls her back.

"You said I died and you did nothing. Who resuscitated me?"

Hand on the doorknob Matthews turns her body back towards Jason.

"Margie didn't stop. She began compressions. I didn't think it would help so I stood back and watched. Then you gasped for air like a newborn – it was miraculous."

Matthews stands in silence for a moment, a look of anguish in her eyes. If only I could tell her that she was right. There was no hope– until I intervened to give him more time. Matthews turns the handle and leaves the room.

Jason looks over both the forms and sets them down on the bedside table. He rolls over and switches out the light.

CHAPTER 18

I've been sitting here for hours watching Jason sleep. I can hear the clock ticking above the muffled sound of nurses doing their nightly rounds. I've stayed at my post in this small private room since Matthews left, apart from leaving briefly to collect a spirit from geriatrics. I've been kidding myself that I'm here to oversee his wellbeing, but my mind keeps flashing back to that kiss we shared when he was briefly in my realm. There was something exciting and new, yet familiar about the exchange, something that keeps pulling me back to him. A movement at the door shakes me out of my daydream as Margie comes in to the room. I'm surprised she's here this early because it's barely twilight and the other patients haven't been woken up yet.

She gently nudges him awake, removes the cannula and helps him sit upright.

"I've put a fresh pair of scrubs and a towel at the end of your bed. As soon as you feel able, hop into the shower and get dressed then we'll get you discharged before the morning shift clocks on."

As Margie turns to leave he calls out her name. Margie looks at him and waits.

"Thank you for not giving up on me. Matthews told me."

Margie smiles and comes over to the bed, she brushes his hair away from his face and pecks him on the forehead.

"I'm just glad you're ok. Don't linger – I'll call a cab for you in twenty minutes." Jason nods and she leaves.

Jason hauls himself from the bed and takes a few tentative steps to the bathroom. He pulls the cords on his hospital issued gown and allows the material to fall to the ground. He flicks the shower taps on then turns to gaze at the mirror. He twists the left side of his body to reveal a large bruise on his shoulder and hip, and winces at the evidence of his fall. He groans slightly as he runs his hand over the darkened area.

I move in close to Jason Reeves and look at his reflection, but I'm not interested in the damage his body has sustained. Instead I'm immersed in his face and build - the green of his eyes offsetting his auburn hair and the smooth cream of his skin taut over lean muscles – and I'm reminded of his father. His eyes, nose and jaw line are all Elwood's, but the smattering of freckles on his shoulders and the ginger stubble around his cheeks are all his, and are a little endearing. When I look at Jason, lustful feelings echo through time and capture fragments of distant memories. I place my hand on Jason's back and rest my cheek on his shoulder and breathe deeply the faint masculine scent of old cologne, perspiration and cigarettes through the veil. Jason turns his head to look in my direction, as if he can sense someone near; but he will neither see me, nor feel anything.

"Be glad you're alive Jason. You'll never know how close you came, nor how close you are right now, to Death."

He steps through me and into the steaming shower. I watch the water cascade over his body and the image evokes another memory. I turn from him, push my way through the bathroom door then slump down on the floor outside with my head in my hands as my chest heaves with sobs. I can see Elwood, his eyes filled with sadness. He holds me close, my face is in his hands as he kisses my forehead and whispers words I don't want to hear.

"I'm sorry, I can't keep doing this. I'm being torn into two. I adore you, I can't stop thinking of you, I can't concentrate I'm so consumed with desire for you. But my wife..." Elwood trails off "…I made a commitment to her…"

Elwood begins to let go of me but, like a petulant child, I cling to his waist and plead with him.

"She doesn't give you what you want, she doesn't make you hot the way I do, and…" I lean up and kiss him passionately as I press my pelvis against his, "…she doesn't make you feel like a man the way I do."

He pushes me back gently. "I'm sorry Ava…"

I hear the shower in the next room shut off and am brought back to the present. I need to pull myself together and follow him to find out whether Jason gets safely out of the hospital without arousing suspicion. I'm not sure why I care so much about his life. Maybe, like the nurses I see getting absorbed in daytime soap operas, watching the daily machinations of the staff in this hospital takes me away from my own mundane existence. I need to know that one night of reckless high jinks won't become the scandal that jeopardises a young man's medical career. I take a few deep breaths to settle my chest from heaving with sobs. I feel like my heart has been ripped out – ironic since I hardly remember Elwood; I have so few memories to look back on to remind me that he once loved me.

CHAPTER 19

I watch as Jason slides into the backseat of a cab that has pulled round to a quiet side entrance adjacent to the old hospital. My sense of relief from knowing that Jason has slipped away undetected is counteracted by a pang of guilt as I look towards the old hospital. I can't judge how long it's been since I saw my unresponsive friend, whom I feel drawn to watch over, but it feels like weeks. I follow the path and enter the ancient stone building then take the stairs down to the coma ward in the basement. Walking down the old familiar corridor towards Albert's room I console myself with the knowledge that old Albert wouldn't have missed me – even if he could sense I was there. His vegetative state would have prevented a real life visitor being a remembered presence by his bed, but I feel guilty all the same, much as if I was neglecting an infirm grandparent rotting in an aged-care facility.

I walk into Albert's room and one of the three beds is empty – the one previously occupied by a young man. It's so rare that any of the nurses mention the men in the coma ward, unless one were to wake after being stable for so long, so I can only assume he has passed. It seems a shame that someone so young didn't get the opportunity to live, but I'm comforted by the idea that the young man didn't need my help to pass on, so he must have been ready for what was on the other side. I smile at that thought, assured that his passing was peaceful.

I'm pleased to see that Albert is still here – someone I can keep coming back to for a chat, regardless of whether he can hear me. It's nice to have a sense of constancy – someone familiar who isn't busy with a task. I pick up Albert's withered hand and slip right back into my game of pretend, where I imagine I'm a regular visitor and that Albert can feel my presence, and know that I'm here to visit him, not as Death but as Ava.

"Hello Albert, I hope you are well and that the nurses are keeping you comfortable." I smile at him weakly. "I'm sorry I haven't visited you. It's no excuse, but for once I've been preoccupied with something other than helping others pass on. I did something extraordinary yesterday – I saved someone's life. I'm sure you've heard the nurses whispering about Dr Reeves being admitted last night; he would have died if he didn't have my help."

With the happy news imparted; my mind turned to darker thoughts about Reeves.

"He might have tried to commit suicide, at least that's what Dr Matthews thinks. If he did it was half-hearted. When he left with Nicole that night he didn't look himself – he was distracted and withdrawn – but I wouldn't have thought he was suicidal. The most amazing thing is that as he lay dying I kissed him and I remembered part of my former life. Turns out I was a naughty little home-wrecker!"

I laugh out loud in spite of myself. I look at Albert as if this is a real conversation and I'm looking to see his reaction.

"Before I was... whatever I am now... I used to be intimate with Dr Reeves' father. I don't know whether I actually loved him or not, but I think maybe I did. I may have destroyed his marriage, but at the time I didn't care. Does that make me a bad person?"

Of course he can't respond, but in my mind I see him crinkle his brow and shake his head in disappointment.

"Their marriage must have mended well enough, or else they wouldn't have had Jason. I think the person I was then was very different to who I am now, though occasionally they cross over and I'm overcome with feelings and objectives that wouldn't ordinarily enter my thoughts. My mind is becoming clouded with memories, feelings, and a new sense of promiscuity that is empowering. I kissed Niklaus for Christ sakes!"

Letting go of Albert's hand I lean back into the chair and ponder.

"I enjoyed it. It felt so good being in his arms feeling him pressed against me when we kissed, I couldn't stop. I enjoyed controlling him, making him moan."

A wicked smile stretches my lips as I reflect, then I snap back into reality, shake my head and laugh.

"I must be unnatural, Albert. To enjoy tormenting Death himself! Enticing him to fixate on me more than he does already. I could be like naughty nurse Nicole and taunt Niklaus by dancing naked..."

My mind's eye sees a swirl of fluttering coloured silk that reveals Niklaus lounging on white linen sheets holding a glass of red wine.

"Shall I dance for you, sir?" I say mockingly while clothed only in undergarments and swirling a piece of Chinese red silk around me. His eyes are mesmerised by the long-haired brunette spinning rhythmically in front of him. She falls dizzily at his feet; he laughs, sets down his glass and lifts the girl's face to his own and kisses her.

Bah! I stand up abruptly with my hands clenched into fists – I keep getting these little flashes like whispers of a previous life, small things like a familiar smell, a vision of a place or a mannerism that's echoed through to the present. It's uninvited and it's getting worse. It was bad enough when the visions were of my recent life, but these whispers feel like they're centuries old and are such a tease!

With a deep breath I try to calm myself.

"Do you want me to help him pass on?"

I jerk my head around, though I already know who it is. Niklaus is standing at the base of the bed looking at Albert.

"No thank you, it's not his time." I'm caught off guard by his sudden appearance, but manage to keep my voice controlled and polite.

"Sometimes it doesn't have to be. Occasionally, you can tip the balance, so long as it doesn't affect another person or a major event."

"Is that what you tried to do with Jason? Try and tip the balance?"

"Dr Reeves should have died, Ava."

I stand in silence. Niklaus walks around the bed and looks down at Albert again.

"He's going to be trapped inside himself for a long while yet, and he'll never come out the coma. I could pull his soul out right now, although it would be cracked from the decay of being trapped, but at least he could move on. Souls need to live and achieve or they begin to collapse upon themselves."

"But I've come to feel like Albert is a friend of mine. I'm not ready to let him go." I know it sounds lame but it's all I've got.

"Come," he says. "I want to show you something." Niklaus holds out his hand and I take it. Without even blinking I find we're suddenly in the children's oncology ward.

CHAPTER 20

All of the lights are out except one in the corner of the room. Niklaus places his hand on my lower back and pushes me gently towards the light. A woman sits beside the bed, holding the hand of a small, frail child. Her head rests on the side of the bed, her eyes are closed and her breathing is slow and rhythmic. From the corner of the room I hear a snort and see a man, presumably the father, is dozing in the corner of the room, his body awkwardly slumped in the hospital visitor chair. I'm surprised to see it's pitch black outside the window – it seems time moves a little differently when I'm in Niklaus's company. I feel Niklaus's hand on my shoulder, and turn to look up at him. He indicates with his eyes towards the sleeping child then moves closer to the bed and he rests a hand on the cool, clammy forehead.

I can't hear any TING, but I can smell a faint muskiness emanating from the child. It's a smell that makes me feel uncomfortable; it makes me want to move away. I scrunch up my nose as it wafts over to me.

"Unpleasant isn't it?" Niklaus says.

"That's coming from the child?"

Niklaus nods.

"Can they smell it too?" I indicate to the man and woman.

Niklaus shakes his head. "People can't smell it, though they can sense it at times." His voice is hushed, even though I'm the only one who can hear him.

Niklaus's hand, as he places it across the child's chest, almost spans the width of the fragile torso. He pulls gently and withdraws the spirit from its vessel, thin blue strands of glowing silk still clinging to the body. The spirit appears cracked, like ancient pottery, looking as though it might crumble at any moment.

"This soul was left to decay in a previous life. Sometimes it's better to detach it, by force if necessary, than to let it linger too long. The damage to this spirit was so severe that it destroyed its new body."

"How can it be mended?" I asked.

"This one can't be. It's too far gone. The best I can do is rip this spirit up so its energy can be absorbed, renewed and redistributed. When this happens, it's a true death, Ava. That man in the coma ward would thank you if he could for releasing his essence so he might try again before he ends up like this." Niklaus gestures to the child in the bed.

I look around the room at the other sleeping children "Are all these children damaged spirits?"

"No, certainly not. Sometimes it's just unlucky genetics. There are more signs to look for than just a physical illness."

"Like that smell?"

Niklaus nods. "Little cracks in a spirit can usually heal in a lifetime, and can even cause a person to flourish creatively or logically. Galileo had little cracks in his soul; he discovered the earth was not flat like once thought and when he presented his findings he was imprisoned. His social prowess was one of his short-comings due to the cracks in his spirit, but his open minded thinking and intelligence was a benefit of it."

"So, it's a double edged blade. Did his soul recover?" I ask.

"Yes, but it took two lifetimes. Do you really want that for your friend?"

I think for a moment before responding.

"It's just not fair... it doesn't feel right killing him like that, but I don't want him to suffer in the next life either."

He listens but doesn't respond to me. He just stands there looking at me while holding the diaphanous life-force loosely in his hands.

"You're sure Albert will never wake up?"

"I'm certain." Niklaus says.

"Will you show me how?" Niklaus looks baffled, so I continue. "I want to be the one to help him cross over." I take a deep, ragged breath and wipe away a tear that has spilled down my cheek.

"All right."

I stand near the child and with Niklaus behind me whispering instructions I cut the strands of blue silk with a wave of my hand then Niklaus tears the soul into pieces by grasping at the feathery wisps of energy and forcibly tearing the spirit at odd angles. It falls to pieces like gossamer fabric, dispersing into clouds that waft and disappear before hitting the ground. I turn away, not because I'm disinterested in the process, but because as old as that spirit might be, I can only imagine the small, sickly child that lay before me. The monitors begin to sound and bleep, the mother wakes with a start and begins screaming for a doctor. My eyes are drawn back to the tragic scene as medical staff burst into the room, and a sense of sadness sinks into my core.

Niklaus takes my hand and pulls me out of the ward. "Ava we don't have to stay. You don't need to see this."

He leads me to the lift and pushes through the veil to press the up button. When the doors glide open we step in. I can't help imagine what thoughts must be going through that woman's mind. After months of feeling that little body growing inside her, pushing him out into this world, nurturing and caring and dreaming of his future, only to see his life force snatched away prematurely. Repossessed by us.

"What are you thinking about?" Niklaus asks.

"I just realised something. I'm never going to be anyone's mother."

"You never have been." Niklaus replies as we reach the roof.

"Pardon?"

"For as long as I've known you, you've never been a mother. You have the capability to fall pregnant and it has happened in the past."

Niklaus pauses for moment. His hands are drawn behind him, one hand wraps around his wrist. It tenses and his hand balls into a fist momentarily. His eyebrows bunch and his expression is pained. He looks to the side, away from me for a moment. Hiding his face.

"Are you all right, Niklaus?"

I touch his shoulder lightly, unsure of what's going on with him, and how I should respond if he bursts into tears or an angry rage. I have no idea what to do with an angry, crying immortal.

Niklaus releases his wrist. Giving his head a gentle shake, as if this action would throw off any unwanted feelings like a dog throwing off water after its been washed, he then runs a hand through his hair smoothing the loosened locks back into place. Readjusting his cuffs and coat, the glimmer of hurt is gone and replaced with the steely, confident and unmoveable statue I've come to know.

"I'm fine." Niklaus pushes aside his coat and sinks his hand into his pocket giving himself a casual presentation. He makes a non-committal shrug then continues, "You seem to always die young. Don't ask me why because I don't know."

I'm desperate to know more but I can tell Niklaus is emotionally connected to this memory. And it something to do with a pregnancy. Could I have fallen pregnant and lost Niklaus's baby? Surely not – how could Death procreate? I need to stay on this subject but not ask outright.

"Do you know how many lives have I had?"

Niklaus shrugs. "A few. Though you spend quite a bit of time on the other side in-between each of them." Niklaus offers me a cigarette and I accept. He lights it for me, though he doesn't light one for himself.

I draw deeply on the cigarette and let this new information settle within me. Ordinarily I would have asked a million questions about all my past lives: What decades had I lived in? How did I look? How did I die? But instead just one question remains in my head – a question that has been burning a hole in my conscious thoughts.

"Niklaus, did I love you in another life?"

Niklaus leans forward and rests his weight on his elbows, rubbing the side of one finger as if to wipe away a speck of dirt.

"Yes."

Recalling the flickers of memories that have been playing over in my head recently, I tentatively offer only those I'm sure of. "I had long, wavy brown hair... and I think we met in a carriage."

Niklaus's eyebrows shoot up in surprise. "Yes! You were on your way to meet your betrothed. That was at least 200 years ago."

"My betrothed?" I'm unable to disguise the surprise in my voice.

"What else do you remember?' Niklaus has an unfamiliar sense of urgency in his voice that shows me this is important to him.

"Nothing tangible, but I see things that I feel are whispers from the past. I don't even know when or what we talked about when we met."

"We spoke about your betrothed. You were fifteen or so, a wealthy merchant's daughter and you were being married to a viscount for a title in exchange for farming land and money as your dowry. Your father wanted a higher social standing and had excess wealth to buy it.'

"Did I love him?"

"You didn't even know him. You'd only met twice before you

were wed."

"Why were you there?" I asked.

"I wanted to know what humanity was really like. It's a common bargain we make as angels of death. The veil gets lowered and we get to experience humanity for a season. The first thing we do is try to assimilate. I saw your carriage from the roadside and you were the first person to see me in my mortal guise, so I followed you."

"So I could have been anyone and you would have followed them?"

Niklaus chuckles to himself. "Well yes, I suppose. But it was because of the way you looked at me and smiled. I felt something foreign, something human for the first time."

"Because of whatever happened in that carriage ride... is that why you love me now?"

"Not exactly, there's more to it than that." He moves closer to me and brushes back a fallen strand of hair off my face. "I've been chasing the ghost of our affair for centuries. Longing to recapture what was lost."

"You know I don't love you now, don't you Niklaus?"

"Yes, but I believe your affection for me will grow in time. You loved me once..."

I sense that perhaps he's right. The person I am now doesn't love him, but the past is niggling at me and sometimes I'm overwhelmed by feelings for Niklaus when a memory from that time engulfs me.

"Spirits grow and adapt to the environment around them; each time they live a new life they forget their old ones. The woman I fell in love with keeps getting further and further away from me with each life you live," Niklaus admits with a sense of desolation in his voice.

I snuff out the cigarette in the gravel and exhale the last of the smoke. "But when I'm in this state I can sense my lives if something triggers a response. Both you and Jason trigger responses and I can see a little into the past. Grasping at the memories I had with you is much harder though, I can only get pieces or sometimes feelings… this is likely as you said, because it was further back than previous lives."

"Ava, can I kiss you?"

I look up at Niklaus, surprised by the timid tone of his voice. He leans in and kisses my cheek, he lingers there a moment and begins to pull away. A flutter of my heart betrays me and I want to kiss him properly so I lean a little closer to him, closing the gap between our bodies. His lips brush mine, and finding no resistance, they linger there, giving me light little kisses that make me crave more. His hands move to cup my cheeks and he presses his lips firmer on mine. My tongue instinctively flicks at his lips, giving him the invitation to deepen our connection. There isn't a tingle on my lips or down my spine like there is with Reeves, but it feels good, and it kindles my desire. The kiss breaks and Niklaus is breathing heavily.

"Tell me you love me, Ava. You don't have to mean it, I just want to hear it."

Niklaus kisses me again then pauses, waiting for me to say it. I can't. Instead I undo his shirt buttons but remove nothing, I just run my hands across his body then kiss his collarbone and his neck.

He seems to enjoy my affections for a moment, but his body doesn't relax.

"I'm must go soon, Ava. Do you want me to be there when you help your friend pass over?"

I pull away from him a little, and he takes the opportunity to fasten his buttons. If it was his intention to kill my passion he has succeeded. I draw a deep breath and let it out slowly.

"I don't know. I feel like I know Albert, even though he never responds to me. It's not like helping a stranger move on."

Niklaus acknowledges my feelings by nodding gently. "It's your decision, but I want you to try to imagine being buried alive; his soul has been screaming on the inside for too many years and now it has begun to crack and decay. Soon there will be nothing left but a fragile essence that will not survive in the next life. He's likely to be weak, sickly – physically or mentally."

"You say it like it's merciful."

"Truthfully, it is. As much as you want to think that I'm an evil entity, I'm necessary. Humans can't continue to evolve as a society if they're immortal. They would be stuck in a way of thinking and they themselves would lose the lust for life."

Niklaus puts his hands on my upper arms and comes in close. "Come on, it's time." He takes my hand then pulls me in closer, wrapping me up in his arms we disintegrate into the blackness to where Niklaus wants us to go.

CHAPTER 21

We appear in the long corridor that leads to Albert's room. Niklaus pulls me by the hand and we glide through the dark silence until we're both standing at the foot of Albert's bed.

I grasp Albert's hand and say to Niklaus, "I don't want his soul torn up. Even if it's damaged."

Niklaus gives me a look of slight consternation, then nods, knowing he won't change my mind about this.

"What happens if I just leave him like this? Maybe he'll wake up one day?"

Niklaus looks over the body and shakes his head, "If you leave him he'll have to be torn up later. His soul will wither as his body dies. Once torn up he'll be dispersed back into the universe; his energy could reoccur at any time in humanity's timeline – past present or future. But it'll need time to heal first, and that could take centuries."

"So, I'm never going to see him again?" I ask.

"No, it's not likely. Most souls continue along the timeline, once they're on the other side they can remember all the lives they've lived, having previously lived in the past they're able to go back if they want. This soul may want to relive the decades he missed out on."

"Will I get to pass on to the other side Niklaus?"

Niklaus seems caught off guard by this question. "I don't know. I don't even know if you'll get an afterlife. I don't know of anyone being stuck like you before."

"If you really loved me you'd try to get me out of here."

Niklaus clears his throat and looks down at his feet. "But I don't want to." His voice is so soft, I can barely hear him. He looks up at me and says, "I'm sorry."

"No, you're not Niklaus. You don't know what this existence is like."

"I can imagine."

"I think you should go Niklaus. I want to say goodbye to Albert before I do it."

Without even looking back I know Niklaus is gone.

Still holding Albert's withered hand, I talk to him one last time about all that has happened in the hospital. I tell him I kissed Dr Reeves junior and that it evoked visions of Dr Reeves Senior. I share the significance of remembering that little piece of my former self and how it changed my outlook on being trapped within this hospital. I mutter my thanks to him for being the one constant that I've been able to keep coming back to, and I hope my visits have given him some comfort. I look at his familiar face one last time then stand over him and reach into his chest and pull. It's much harder work than the usual reaping, because this person isn't on the edge of death, but Albert's soul comes out of his body and now he is young again, with only a few gashes on his soul, but nothing compared some others I've helped pass over. While holding onto his soul I sever the blue silk that still anchors him to his body. The machines around him begin to whoop and screech. Once released from its body, his essence takes on the form of a young man in a military uniform. I lead him away into the corridor, to save our ears from the assault of the alarms, so that I can say my final goodbyes. I look at him and open my mouth to speak but he interjects.

"Thank you for watching over me all these years. It was like I had my own guardian angel."

"You could sense I was here?"

He nods. "I enjoyed hearing about everything that was happening in the hospital. It was the only distraction I had from the misery of being trapped inside myself."

Relief washes over me and I feel blessed that I was able to give some comfort to him.

"I want tell you something. About you."

I feel perplexed. "About me?"

"About the day you died. I was there."

Fearing that the afterlife will take him too soon I snatch at his hands. "Tell me!"

"You were my nurse during the war. You were caring for me before I became unconscious. I was badly injured and you were taking down my information. That's why you know my name is Albert. Albert Abbernathy. I was muttering my name to you when you were shot."

I can see a glimmer of light over his shoulder and I squeeze his hands tight. "What happened?"

Albert seems to sense the urgency in my voice, and speaks in a rush. "A man in the bed opposite awoke in a panic and thought he was still on the field. There were soldiers everywhere – it was chaos. He grabbed the gun from the officer who was assigned to watch over him and shot at random. You were hit and so was an orderly. His wound was superficial, but yours was fatal."

I search Albert's face and try to dredge up memories. I remember the blood splatter hitting Albert's face. My blood. I remember seeing his panicked face as I fell to my knees. The next thing I remember is waking in the corridor outside of the ward with Niklaus's hand on my thigh, and screaming as he dragged me further down the corridor. His attempts to console me. My fear and panic at what I thought was harassment. Nothing was going to comfort me at that time. Nobody could see me and I could touch nothing. I cried, screamed and fought against Niklaus for hours until I was exhausted and nothing made sense.

The light is getting brighter, and forming the shape of a portal. I can sense Albert is resisting looking behind him. He looks at me with an intensity that I don't expect. "I don't know how you ended up like this – why you assumed Death's role, but I want to help you."

My heart jumps. "Help me? How?"

Albert shakes his head. "I don't know yet. I don't know what's on the other side, but when I get there I'll do something for you if I can."

My heart sinks a little. "If you can remember to help me, that is. Once you see the light..."

Albert grips my hands. "Because of you these gashes in my soul aren't deep. I wasn't left idle for decades. I had company that kept me from screaming from within. I want to help you as you have helped me."

From the fully formed portal comes a chorus of cheers, with streamers and confetti falling out of the light and evaporating once it touching the ground on this side. A hero's homecoming. Albert stands stiffly and salutes me. I give a haphazard salute in reply. "On your way solider." I say with a sad smile.

Albert turns and marches into the light and I am left in a dark corridor with tears running down my face.

The whine of the machines around Albert's body seep back into my conscious mind. The nurses' station is at the end of the corridor, and only one nurse is usually stationed at it. He's a big burly man who rarely has to minister to his patients on this ward. I take a seat beside Albert's bed and wait for the nurse on duty to respond. He pokes his head in and presses the emergency buzzer and begins a half-hearted attempt at CPR. I sit back and watch as the on-call doctor pronounces Albert's frail body dead. I see the burly nurse prepare Albert's body so that it can be moved to the morgue by an orderly. The nurse strips the bed, wipes the machinery down and packs it away. Within a few hours it's like Albert was never there.

I've known this day was coming but I don't cry like I thought I would. I just sit and watch as everything connected with Albert's existence is removed from the room. I stand and leave, knowing I did the right thing, and that Albert is in a better place.

CHAPTER 22

I drift along the hospital corridors with Albert on my mind. It's comforting that someone else knows about my predicament, and it's nice he wants to help me, but I don't know how he can. Although I can't remember being on the other side, I can't imagine it being a place of business where people can seek out a customer service representative. I like to imagine it's a place where every whim is catered for; a place to relax and regroup before deciding when to reintegrate into the timeline and begin again in another life. As I wander I hear raised voices coming from the car park in front of me. I look over and see Jason and Nicole arguing. I'm too far away to hear the details, so I mosey on over to listen in.

Jason's arms are flailing around in agitation. "I could have lost my job, Nicole! It could have been the end of my career!"

"You're not a kid anymore, Jason! You're responsible for your own decisions. If you want to do pills you can't blame other people when it doesn't work out for you." Nicole crosses her arms across her chest.

"Shhh! Keep your voice down." Jason's finger darts to his mouth.

"Don't shush me, Reeves. You came to me. You wanted to party. I was fine with just dancing and having a couple of drinks."

"You're unbelievable!" Jason throw his arms in the air.

"Why? Because you're looking for someone to blame? What was I supposed to do? Just let you die on the dance floor?"

"You could have asked the ambulance to take me to another hospital," Jason hisses.

"We were forty minutes away from the next hospital. You could have died in that time, Jason."

"I know that!"

"Then why are you still yelling at me?!"

"Because this looks bad!"

"Looks bad?" Nicole cocks her eyebrow. "It could look a whole lot worse. At least you've got Matthews covering your arse. You could have been pulled up on disciplinary charges if they had drug tested you. Or you could have died."

Jason releases his puffed up chest and slumps. "Yeah, I know." Jason swivels his body round to lean on the side of the car. He's looking off into the distance. "Look, Nicole. I don't think we should see each other anymore; you seem to bring out the worse in me. I've got some stuff I need to work through by myself and while I'm around you I won't do that. I seem to be spiralling out of control."

Nicole takes a sharp breath as she unfolds her arms then her face contorts as if to form a response. She halts, pushes out her breath in a turbulent force then turns on her heel and struts off in the direction of her scooter.

Reeves leans against his beaten up car and watches her go. His hand draws out a packet of cigarettes from his pocket, which he lifts to his lips to pull out a cigarette with his mouth. He lights the cigarette with the time-stricken Zippo that once belonged to Dr Reeves Senior. The metal glints momentarily as it catches the security lighting. I walk over and lean beside Jason while he draws on his cigarette. I notice Jason smokes Marlboro and I have a little flicker of recollection that Reeves Senior smoked Chesterfields during the war. Even though this moment is different, I have a sense of déjà vu. I lean my head on Jason's shoulder and my mind flickers back to a similar moment in time with Elwood. In my imagination I can feel the hot sun on my face and the heat radiating off the concrete before I open my eyes to darkness of the night and I'm alone in the car park. Jason Reeves has already left and dawn is winking over the horizon.

CHAPTER 23

I amble from the car park back into the hospital and find a comfortable place to sit. I close my eyes and tilt my head to the ceiling. I'm still mulling over Albert and hoping he's alright. It's sinking in that now he's gone I have nowhere to go; nobody to talk to, apart from Niklaus, of course, but his appearances are unpredictable and out of my control. I make a concerted effort to sort through my thoughts, remembering little titbits that have been left behind from my previous lives.

'We can take it!' – the unofficial motto of the British during the Second World War.

I recall having the weekend off work after getting clearance from the ward sister to visit my mother in the East End. An air raid during dinner. People heading to shelters, either in back yards or underground train stations. Trying to persuade my mum to leave the house and take refuge in the neighbours' bomb shelter, but because of the incidences of looters during raids, she refused to leave her possessions and freshly gathered rations. Hiding under the kitchen table and praying. My mum's poky kitchen with the yellow drapes over the window. I remember being exhausted after a long shift at the hospital and falling into a restless sleep in my mother's lap; her stroking my hair as the bombs rained down around us. It's bizarre how you can become accustomed to any kind of chaos. I remember the dust over the table when the raid was over.

When I reflect back on that memory, I realise something is different: My eyes are now open to someone I didn't know was there before. I see a dark figure and I know his face. Niklaus. At the time I didn't know he was there, but I now realise Niklaus was watching over me that night while I took shelter under the kitchen table. Watching, without the intent to reap the souls of the deceased, but rather like a guardian angel. Unable to change what was occurring he could only wait to see if I was to die that night. If I had died that night he would have been there waiting for me.

"Excuse me lady?" a small voice squeaks.

I tilt my head down and a look into the eyes of a small bald child who is looking directly at me.

"Yes?"

"You're the lady who was here a few nights ago, aren't you? With the man..."

I look around and realise I'm in a caregiver's seat in the children's oncology ward. Two beds down from where I'm sitting is where the spirit of the small child was harvested by Niklaus.

"Yes".

"He's dead now."

I rise from the chair to walk towards her and stand at the end of her bed.

"They say I'm going to die soon." The child speaks in a matter of fact way that makes me think she doesn't understand the weight of her words.

"No, you're not." I say to her with a warm smile. Funny how we have automatic responses in these situations. I glide across the floor towards the ward door and mutter to myself. "Well not yet anyway."

CHAPTER 24

Margie sits on an overturned milk crate on the roof with a cigarette in her hand. Nicole stands to her left, arms crossed over her chest, only uncrossing them to draw on the cigarette she has hanging from her mouth.

Nicole looks a lot less glamorous than the last time I saw her – I'm guessing it's the end of her shift because her makeup is smudged under her tired eyes.

"I suppose you heard it's over," she says to Margie. "We had a huge argument last week in the carpark. Prick! He's been avoiding me ever since."

"Do you still have feelings for him?"

"I don't know how I feel about him, Margie. I'm upset, but that could be because he's blaming me for what happened."

"Do you think you're to blame?"

Nicole scoffs. "Of course not! He's an adult who's responsible for his own decisions." Nicole draws on her cigarette as she looks at the fob watch attached to her scrubs.

The door to the roof swings open and Reeves steps through the breech. His eyebrows peak in surprise as he sees Nicole and he hesitates. He looks down at his cigarettes.

Nicole exhales forcefully.

"Relax Reeves, I'm going." Nicole stamps towards the door and pushes past him.

Reeves jumps back from the door and allows her passage. Reeves then looks towards Margie. Margie smiles and gestures towards an empty milk crate beside her. Reeves walks over and takes a seat.

"You can't avoid her forever, Reeves."

"I know, but I don't know what to say to her yet."

"She thinks it's over."

Reeves lights his cigarette and draws deeply on it. On his exhaling breath he says, "It is. But I think I should talk to her. We didn't end on the best of terms."

"Nicole thinks you're blaming her for what happened."

Reeves shifts uncomfortably. "Yeah, that probably wasn't a good idea, but it seemed accurate at the time. I felt like if she had said no to going out clubbing, none of this would have happened."

"But it did happen, and now you have to deal with the consequences."

Reeves chews on his bottom lip. He looks across to Margie. "There won't be any consequences."

Margie's hand had raised part way to her mouth with her cigarette, but it remains poised.

"I'm assuming Nicole told you what happened that night?"

Margie nods.

Reeves runs his hand through his hair, and his eyes look off towards the smattering of cityscape buildings in the distance. He looks down at his feet and his voice is hushed.

"Can I please ask that you don't say anything to any other staff members? I want to put it behind me, and if it gets out that Dr Matthews covered for me, you wouldn't just be ruining my career, but hers as well."

"Did she forge the incident report?"

Reeves falls silent. He draws on his cigarette before continuing. "She took care of everything."

"What about Nicole? What if she says something?"

"I don't think she will. That night doesn't put her in a good light either." Reeves looks at Margie and his eyes are pleading. "When I was with Nicole she helped me blow off some steam and relax. I didn't feel so pressured to succeed, but she's a hedonist and brings out the worst in me."

Margie interjects. "Is that why you broke it off?"

"Partly. I was spinning out of control, but it was only when I died I realised I had to end it. I'll talk to her soon and give her some closure, but I need a little time to figure out how to word it."

Margie nods. "Perhaps a frank discussion about her behaviour and how it influences others is what she needs. If you want my opinion, you need to find less self-destructive methods of relaxation. I know people have a preconception about you because of your father, but don't feel pressured to live up to his image."

Reeves takes a last drag on his cigarette then leans forward and stubs it out in the ashtray on the pilfered waiting room table. He leans back on his milk crate and looks at her.

"What happened to my dad, Margie?"

"What do you mean?"

"Everyone says he was a great doctor. The youngest head of the department who lost his passion and drive. I've heard a few conflicting stories, but you were there and my dad won't talk about it."

"Yeah, I'm not surprised." Margie mutters so quietly I'm not sure if Reeves has heard her.

"Is it because he lost a patient?"

Margie scoffs.

"What?"

"Do you really want to know, Jason?"

"I wouldn't be asking unless I wanted to know."

Margie stubs out her cigarette with unnecessary force into the ashtray and the table wobbles. She reaches for her packet and lights another. She inhales deeply before answering.

"Your father was an average doctor. With influence. I'm not meaning to be insulting, but his legacy has been inflated since his departure."

"What do you mean?" Reeves' hands reach for his cigarette packet and lighter.

"During the war this hospital was run by the military. Your mother's family influenced the board of directors to advance Elwood's career to Department Head so he couldn't be shipped overseas to serve on the front line."

"How do you know that?"

"I'm one of the longest servicing staff members in this hospital. I knew a reliable source at the time who told me. I haven't breathed a word about it since I found out."

"So do you know what happened with my dad's patient? The one he lost?"

Margie stares at the bright embers at the end of her cigarette and seems fascinated by the way they are turning into light grey ash. Reeves tilts his head towards her and it looks like he's unsure whether he still has her attention. Margie looks at Reeves and draws on her cigarette. As she exhales, she speaks softly.

"I know exactly what happened. I was there. And I'm uniquely acquainted with the details. But Jason, once I tell you, I can't untell you. The story with all its details doesn't cast your father in the best light."

Reeves seems to consider this. I watch as he turns over Elwood's beaten old zippo lighter in his hand. "I want to know the truth. Warts and all."

Margie nods. "Your father was having an affair."

She draws on her cigarette again, giving Reeves a moment to absorb the information he's just heard. Reeves doesn't seem surprised. Perhaps he had considered his father's infidelity already? Or heard a piece of vicious gossip that had been passed down from staff member to staff member through the years, each time becoming more contorted and embellished.

Margie continues. "But it wasn't with a patient – it was a nurse."

Margie searches Jason's face, seeming to look for an indication that she should hold back on the details. Jason doesn't give her any.

"She was my best friend. We met during the war when single women were being called into service to be trained as nurses. We were roomed together when the hospital still had dormitories."

Reeves nods as he turns the lighter over between his fingers. "How did it start?"

I racked my brain trying to force a memory to come forth, I can remember the affair but not how it started. I sit on an empty overturned milk crate and lean forward so I can catch every word that Margie is relaying to Jason, hoping that something might spark a memory.

"They would pass each other in the hallways and stop to chat to each other when the ward sister was preoccupied. Chatting became flirting, then one day Elwood asked her to go for a drink with him at the end of her shift."

It was raining. I can remember that. I wore the best dress I owned – brown with embroidered flowers on the skirt. I had borrowed a pair of Margie's new brown heels, as all of my shoes where old and practical. Not appropriate for trying to impress a handsome young doctor. Hitler didn't make an appearance that night – no bombs rained down over London – and I can recall thinking it was a sign. It was a chaste evening. As Elwood and I talked, his features were animated while his eyes looked more alive than I had ever seen at the hospital. He was attentive and respectful. When we left the public house and he escorted me back to the dormitories, he kissed my cheek and his lips lingered on my skin until I pulled away, embarrassed, because of the heat my flesh was giving off.

"How long did the affair last?" Reeves asks Margie.

"A little over a year."

Reeves contemplates the information. The cigarette in his hand is laden with ash. He flicks it off then turns to her. "Did he love her?"

My breath catches in my throat. I know that I loved Elwood, but I have no memory of him saying he loved me back. Thankfully, Margie is quick with a response. "I think he did. Nobody is that distraught over someone's death if they didn't love them."

"Was he going to leave my mum?"

"No, Ava and Elwood had broken up at the time she was shot. They parted ways because Elwood was still in love with your mother and wouldn't leave her."

Something in what Margie said didn't ring true. A memory flickered into being and came to me with such clarity that it could have happened yesterday.

Margie and I had been drinking gin and tonic in our room until we ran out of tonic, but by then we were enjoying ourselves and didn't want to stop. Margie had brought a radio with her to the nurses' home, and I recall the sound of The Andrew's Sisters playing in the background as we spoke.

"I saw Dr Reeves looking at you on the ward today. Is there something you want to tell me, Ava?" Margie's voice was teasing, not interrogating, and her slender figure was gyrating to the music as her signature red lips drew effortlessly on her cigarette.

"No, no... there's nothing to tell. He said it was over and we should leave it at that."

"Well that look he gave you was not a look of a man who wants things to be over. I think if you give him a few days to himself he'll come crawling back to you."

After I took a sip of gin I replied. "Well, what's the point, Margie? He's married. It's not like he's going to leave his wife for me."

"You never know, he might."

"No, he says he's committed to her."

"Is that why is he dallying with you? Committed with her but smitten with you? He probably doesn't want to give up the weight that his wife's family throws around."

"Or the money," I said, followed by a snide cackling laugh that I hoped covered up the hurt I felt.

I review every memory I have of Elwood. I can recall little mention of his relationship with his wife. Something deep inside of me tells me that he didn't love her; that it was a marriage of convenience. Perhaps that's what I wanted to believe at the time of our affair.

"Ava." Reeves rolls my name around his mouth; the way he pronounces it makes it seem like a foreign name to him. "You said she was shot?"

Margie nods. "By a patient. It was quick and instant. Your father said he'd never seen someone die so fast from a gunshot wound before. By the time her body hit the ground she was dead. Your father went to her and tried to staunch the bleeding wound, but there was no life to save. She was gone and I saw the anguish in your father's face. Men didn't cry in those days, the hurt that he felt was quickly stopped up. He left her body on the ground and excused himself."

"What did you do?"

"I followed him into the men's bathroom. He maintained his composure as he washed her blood off his hands. I touched his shoulder. I remember the way he jumped in surprise when he recognised it was me, then he crumbled. We had never spoken, except formally, but he knew that I was aware of the affair. He cried and I hugged him. From then on he became distracted, and at times, negligent. I think the hardest thing for him was that he had to try and maintain the image of a young, happily married doctor while trying to grieve."

"Did my mum ever find out?"

Margie's eyebrow shoot up and her face is animated. "Yeah,

she did. She approached Ava and me in the street when we were leaving the hospital for a night out."

"What happened?"

As Margie begins to relay the story to Jason, my mind is distracted by a memory. Margie's words become further and further away as I see the side entrance to the hospital, with its heavy wrought iron gates in my mind's eye. I remember a woman in a fur lined coat, leaning against the entrance, smoking a cigarette and looking towards us. At the time Margie and I took no notice of her until we became aware she was following us. Margie stopped and turned to her.

"Can we help you with something ma'am?"

The woman stopped in her tracks a few feet from us both. "Are you the bitch who's sleeping with my husband?" She asked with such calm that she could have been asking for directions.

I stood beside Margie in the street with my heart pounding. This was always the risk of dating a married man.

Margie turned her head to me then back to the woman. "I think you have confused me with someone else." She put her hand on my shoulder and pushed me to walk forwards. We took a couple of steps together before Margie was yanked back by her coat by the woman.

"I think you are the bitch who's sleeping with my husband." The woman spat the words out like venom.

"No, I'm not! Get your hands off me!"

Margie pulled at her coat, trying to get out of the woman's grasp. Margie's coat slipped out of the woman's hands, so she grabbed Margie by the shoulders and shook her.

"I know some slutty little nurse is fucking my husband, and the ward sister said she had the night off tonight and was going out to a dance. I surmise it's you – you look the type!"

Margie's eyes were wide with shock, she seemed unsure as to whether she was dealing with a deranged woman, and whether continuing to protest would do any good. Her stylish blonde hair was being shaken loose in the scuffle, and hair-pins were falling onto the cobblestones

I lurched forward to get in between them and tried to pry the woman off Margie. Margie was wailing and proclaiming her innocence. A huddle of people had stopped across the street to watch the show.

I took a step back from both of them and yelled – "It's me!" My words echoed off the cobbled stones and into the late afternoon.

The woman stopped shaking Margie and looked at me in disbelief. Margie looked at me with her mouth wide open in the manner of posing an unasked question. The situation became eerily calm.

"I'm the one having an affair with Dr Reeves." I used his professional title and I don't know why. This was a personal matter.

The woman released Margie who took several steps back from the woman. She began to straighten her clothing and pat her hair, regaining some of her composure. Mrs Reeves looked me up and down. I was wearing my best dress with old shoes and a fairly worn coat. We stood eye to eye, the contrast of our social standing more apparent than ever. I felt a sharp sting across my cheek. It was so fast I barely saw her hand move. Remembering it now I can still feel the brute force of the impact her hand made as it struck my face, knocking my head sideways.

"Stay away from my husband. I won't warn you again." There was a moment of silence as I absorbed the shock. Mrs Reeves pushed past us both and stampeded down the street. We heard the muttering dispersal of the onlookers but we didn't move until the clicking of her heels was no longer audible.

When I snap back into reality Reeves doesn't look shocked upon hearing about his mother's behaviour. I surmise that Margie must have omitted some details. I only catch the tail end of her story because I was lost in my own recollection. We had gone to the dance, but the entire night felt somewhat deflated since the incident, and I apparently sported a large hand mark across my face for a few hours that powder barely covered.

Reeves stubs out his cigarette, exhaling the last of the smoke through his nose.

"If she hadn't died, do you think they would have gotten back together?"

Margie pauses for a long moment. She puffs on her cigarette to make the pause seem natural, then stubs out the ember before replying.

"We can never know for sure. It's not something I've given much thought to. I believe that things such as this work themselves out for a reason."

A quintessential non-answer. Margie is trying her best to justify everyone's actions and be an impartial informant, but her nurturing nature seems to want to protect Jason from nefarious details that would cast shadows over his parents' characters.

CHAPTER 25

When Jason smiles he looks incredibly handsome and I understand why women fall for him. I find myself being among those women at times, but thankfully I don't have to hide my adoration. There are benefits to being invisible I suppose. I can be so close to him sometimes, like when he's sleeping in the on-call room. I can lay beside him and gaze into his sleeping face. That's how my time is being spent these days. I'm aware that I'm replacing Albert with Reeves, but there's a void inside me that I need to fill. I follow him closely and watch him interact with patients and staff. I speak to him intimately, as though we're colleagues or friends, even though I know he can't hear me. I stroke his cheek affectionately, though he can't feel me. This is how I exist now, just being close to Reeves, and reliving the kiss we shared together a thousand times over in my head. But still this idolisation doesn't fulfil me, it makes me instead feel longing for someone who can hear and touch me. The world has somehow become lonelier since I've started becoming infatuated with Dr Jason Reeves.

Today is one of those days that is filled with a sense of longing, just being close to Reeves isn't enough to satiate me. You'd think that by closing my eyes I'd escape briefly, but whenever I do I have visions of being with Elwood Reeves. My clit has a pulse and is yearning to be appeased. I think it's been many months since I saw Niklaus. Although I've always felt alone here, lately the intensity has increased and my body is physically reacting to this need for physical connectivity.

Once, when I was wandering the hospital, I followed a nurse into the ladies' locker room. She was clearing out her pigeon hole. I can't recall whether she was fired or quit, but I knew that she wouldn't be coming back and she was in a rush to leave. As she pulled out her spare shoes, toiletry bag and cardigan, an emerald green bundle of fabric tumbled silently to the floor. With her arms full she turned on her heals and strutted out of the locker room. I watched her retreat, then my eye was drawn to the bundle of green on the floor. I focused and pushed through the veil to pick up the fabric and revealed a sweetheart neckline dress with a full skirt. I increased my concentration and tugged hard at the fabric, pulling it into my domain. As it transitioned, the emerald green colour dissolved and turned into an inky black where my hands held the material. The now black dress belonged to me from that day forth.

As I stand on the roof I'm wearing the pilfered dress and my fingertips clutch at the fabric near my groin. I throw my head back, pent up energy is radiating through me. I groan and roll my neck. It would be so nice to play with Niklaus right now. I'd love to get Niklaus to feel as pent up and frustrated as how I feel right now. With a sly smile, I want to do exactly that. I wander down from the roof, to the quiet corridors, and a passing clock tells me the time is 11pm. The lights in the closest waiting room are off and the hospital has limited staff on the wards. I strip off my thick black trench coat, drop it on the floor then I lay on the bench, the wide black skirt spilling over on either side of the bench. I close my eyes and inhale deeply. As I breathe out I visualise Niklaus, and little flashes come to me from a time before I was a nurse.

My hair is long, wavy and brown. I'm corseted with a chemise and pantaloons covering my body. I'm smiling and so is Niklaus, we're looking into each other's eyes while I'm straddled on top of him. My fingertips are clutching his shirt and I can see myself kissing him. His hand comes to my face and he deepens the kiss while wrapping his other arm around my waist. I have a warm feeling of safety being in his arms and a wish to be immortal so I can be with him forever.

I open my eyes with a jolt and sit up straight on the bench. I realise that is what Niklaus has been chasing – the ghost of me.

"Niklaus," I whisper.

With a cool breeze he's standing there before me. There's a question burning inside me.

"Have you always been watching over me, like you did when I was at my mother's house and there was an air raid?"

"When you hid under the table?"

I nod.

Niklaus gently nods his head. "Yes. I promised I'd always watch over you, Ava. And you made me promise to be there when you crossed over. So whenever you could have died, I was standing by, waiting for you."

Something in what he says rings true. His word trigger a memory. I remember asking Niklaus something while we were laying together in bed under white linen sheets. Hands clasped together I made him swear that when I died he'd be the one to help me pass on. Not just in that life but in every life.

Niklaus continues. "During the war I was with you a lot, even though you weren't on the front line, there were some close calls. Seeing you almost die over and over again is probably why I tried to push you out of the way when you got shot. I didn't want to see you die again."

Still dazed from reliving tender moments with Niklaus, I stand and walk over to him, slinking my hands under his coat and drawing myself close to him I embrace him in a way that I haven't in centuries.

"Why didn't you tell me that sooner?"

"I didn't think you'd believe me. Better that you remember for yourself."

I rest my cheek on his chest and feel the stiff black material under my cheek. I can feel Niklaus's arms encapsulate me. Just for a moment I long to feel my skin pressed against his. I tilt my head up until my lips are gently brushing the nape of his neck. I press my lips to his collarbone and Niklaus body stiffens in response, I'm not sure whether he's struggling with disbelief or trying to be respectful. The pulse between my legs insists I continue, so I kiss a little higher on his neck. Niklaus seizes the opportunity to take my face in his hand, tilting my face up to him. He looks into my eyes, wordlessly asking permission to proceed. I close my eyes and open my mouth slightly until I feel tentative lips touching mine. He is warm and real. There is no veil dividing us so I relax into the moment and enjoy the sensations. Niklaus's hands move to my face and he deepens his kiss into something more substantial. I moan quietly into his mouth and I lean on him for support as my knees buckle. I haven't been kissed like this since I saved Reeves from the other side.

"What do you want for this?" Niklaus asks, still holding my face between his hands, stroking my cheek with his thumb.

"I don't know. You can owe me one."

Niklaus kisses me again and asks, "How far can I take it?"

I move my hands from Niklaus's waist to his neck and pull him close to me. Instigating a kiss for the first time I then tilt my head and whisper in his ear. "Till I say stop. You had better think of something good to tell me in return."

"What no more questions?" he asks.

"I think I'll get better answers if I leave my questions unknown and open-ended."

"Are you going to let me fill in the blanks for you?"

"Yes. Because what you're telling me is triggering memories. I remembered something, before you blew in." I peck his lips again, then pull away to look into his eyes. I push him towards the bench behind him. I coerce him to sit then straddle his lap. "I remember sitting on top of you like this..." I clutch my hands around the back of his neck, "...and doing this." I lean into the kiss and I deepen it to rival my past memories of this similar moment. With a brief flash the memory is there in my head and gone again within a second. Niklaus places his hand around my waist and pulls me off him slightly. Niklaus is trying to keep his composure but I can see the mask slipping. This is something he's wanted since I've been captive in his domain and he is finally getting what he wants. His breathing is elevated and his cheeks are a little flushed. My cheeks feel as though they're on fire. I can see the beginning of Niklaus's collarbone where I had kissed him earlier still peeking out from under his shirt. I long to feel another person's skin and be touched in return. I slowly begin to unfasten three of his shirt buttons. I open the shirt to reveal smooth alabaster skin beneath. I indulge myself by letting my hand run across the exposed skin up to Niklaus's neck and into his short dark hair. As I lean in for another kiss, Niklaus mutters, "Do you remember what happened next?" His hands travel down from my waist to skim over my buttocks and thighs.

"No," I mutter back. "It was just a little flash and then it was gone."

Niklaus whispers. "Let me remind you..." he kisses me again as he pushes up the black fabric of my dress over my thighs and reaches for my underwear.

The sensation of his hands grappling around my buttocks causes a moment of panic. I pull away from Niklaus's mouth and I unthinkingly exclaim, "Stop!"

I'm wearing the black knee length dress solely for the purpose of having him touch me without revealing too much skin. Old instincts kick in and my sense of control of this situation has almost slipped away.

Niklaus respectfully stops, removing his hands from under my dress, and he reluctantly draws his hands back up to my waist. Pulling back from our close proximity to look into my face he gauges my reaction. I sit back a little on Niklaus's lap, trying to quieten my breathing. He sighs deeply and smooths back his dark hair behind his ear with one hand.

"Too far?" he asks.

"A little. Even though nobody can see us it still feels indecent to be so intimate in a public place."

Niklaus cocks his eyebrow. "It was your idea."

"I know." I look down and I can feel my face flushing.

Niklaus touches my chin and tilts my head back to him. He leans up and kisses me affectionately. After a brief moment of silence, he asks

"Do you feel sparks when we kiss?"

"It's pleasant. It's warm and real."

Niklaus groans quietly. "Yeah, me neither." Niklaus takes his hands off my waist and places them on the bench. He drums his finger briefly then stops. "There used to be a spark when we kissed." He says.

"When we first met?"

"Mmm..." Niklaus murmurs in agreeance. "Sometimes I feel it a little, like just then when you were willing. But it isn't like it used to be." Niklaus puts his hands back on my thighs.

I see the sadness in his eyes. "It must be hard."

"What?" he queries.

"You miss her."

He looks me in the face and shakes his head. "It's you. I miss you."

"But that's not me anymore."

"I know. Every time you died the woman I fell in love with, Avaline, got further and further away. You still have her smile and her laugh, but her mannerisms, way of speaking and poise are gone."

"It was a different time. Everything you miss are learned responses. Enforced behaviours to fit into the time when she was alive."

"It isn't just that. Every time someone dies they'll be reborn, looking similar, but forgetting their past life. Instead they'll carry with them the essence of their past life. Ever wonder why some people have an irrational fear of something but have no rhyme or reason as too why? Someone could have committed suicide and regretted their decision in the last few seconds of their demise, or been pushed off a building in their past life then in their next life they have an irrational fear of heights and can't pinpoint the reason as too why."

Niklaus is silent for a long moment and seems transfixed with touching my skin. He strokes my arms as if to warm me up, even though I don't feel the cold.

"Will you tell me more about her?"

"Avaline?"

"Yes."

Niklaus takes a deep breath and relaxes into the bench. His eyes flicker up as if recalling a memory that has been buried deep.

"It was one of your earlier lives – your soul was still young. Fresh energy bubbling away within. Your father was a wealthy merchant. In order to improve his social setting he had a union arranged for you with a Viscount Harmsworth."

"Harmsworth." The name doesn't ignite any memories. "Was he a nice man?"

"No. He was a libertine and a philanderer. He would seem nice enough to women of a certain standing, but he had little regard for consent of those below him." Niklaus takes my hand in his and he softly kisses my knuckles "We met on the way to his estate."

For a brief second I can see a wide open field covered in snow and a man in a thick black coat on the side of the road. "In a carriage. We stopped in town to change the horses and you got on board."

"Yes! See, you do remember."

"Only bits and pieces. As you were telling me it came to me. But I can't be sure if it was a memory or a dream, or suggestion."

"Old memories feel that way Ava."

Niklaus suddenly falls silent and his body stiffens like a dog on a hunt having picked up the trail of the poor beast it's chasing. "Mmmm..." Niklaus muses to himself. He motions for me to move off his lap and we both stand straight facing each other. Niklaus picks up my trench coat off the floor and slips it over my shoulders. He takes me by the hand and pulls me close to him.

"Come on, I have something to show you that will make up the difference for what you've given me today."

I hold tight to Niklaus as we dissipate into nothingness.

CHAPTER 26

We arrive in a curtained-off section of the Emergency room together. A young woman reclines on a trolley bed while a nurse cleans a gash on her forehead. Her fair hair is matted with blood and her eyes are glazed in confusion, but she chatters to Nurse Susie, who is attending her.

"I can't stay here. My son's still at school. I'm feeling much better now."

"Sorry, Mrs Saunders, but we'll have to keep you here."

"Can I call my husband then? I need to see if he can pick up our son. I was running late. I didn't see the truck enter the intersection."

"We've already called your husband. He's on his way. Just try to relax and let us do our jobs."

"But my son?"

"Everything's been taken care of. Now we just need to take care of you and your baby."

Mrs Saunders' hands reach to her swollen belly.

I look around the ward but can't see any other patients in worse circumstances. I look at Niklaus but his focus is on the pregnant woman on the bed.

I lean over to him and instinctively use a hushed voice. "What are we doing here? I can't hear any bells."

"Ava, death happens all the time. You are only called to spirits that need your help to cross over. You won't hear the bells every time someone passes." Niklaus speaks in his usual tone and I'm reminded there was no need for me to whisper.

"So, is she dying?"

"Not yet, but she may soon. All I can hear right now is a dull ting, it will become louder depending on the choice she makes.

"Choice?"

People make choices every day that have the capacity to change the future for better or worse. Some moments are more significant than others."

"How is this moment significant?"

"It doesn't matter if she dies, but her baby must live. I don't just reap souls. Sometimes I get orders to manipulate a situation to save a life if the future hangs in the balance."

Matthews appears from between the curtains and strides up to the end of the bed. She tucks some paperwork into the back of the chart.

"What's the problem? Why can't I go home?"

Matthews cocks her eyebrow at the chart then looks at the patient. "We've confirmed you have a placental eruption from the trauma to your abdomen from the accident."

The woman tenses and cradles her stomach. "Is my baby going to be ok?"

Dr Matthews takes a consent form on a clipboard from a passing nurse. She closes the chart and places it at the foot of the bed. "We can save you both by delivering your baby via C-section and removing the damaged placenta while we stop the internal bleeding."

"But my baby isn't ready, I'm only 8 months."

"That's still a viable foetus. The baby will be cared for in our neonatal ward and should be fine to come home in a couple of weeks, maybe even less time than that if it's strong enough.

This is the safest option, so long as you're willing to accept blood transfusions."

The patient bursts into tears and looks down at her stomach. "My religion forbids it." The woman leaves her stomach unguarded for a moment as she wipes away tears that had welled in her eyes.

"If you don't opt for surgery, you and the baby are likely to die."

"I know!" the woman cries.

Dr Matthews puts the clipboard on the woman's lap, takes a pen from her breast coat pocket and places it with the board. "Take a moment to think about yourself and your baby. Both of your lives are medically preventable deaths."

The woman sits and thinks for a moment, her chest heaving with repressed sobs. She pushes the clipboard away to feel where her bump is.

"Where's my husband? I need to talk to my husband!"

Nurse Susie puts a reassuring hand on hers and leans over the bed. "We've called him Mrs Saunders. He's on his way."

Matthews is watching the scene with an inscrutable expression as she taps her pen against the reclaimed chart. "Every moment counts Mrs Saunders – we don't have time to wait for him."

Mrs Saunders' eyes look around the room and her arms flail frantically. She can no longer contain her sobs and is on the point of becoming hysterical. I love watching Matthews when she's under pressure like this because I never know which way she's going to react.

"Nurse! Go to the nurses' station and see how far away Mr Saunders is. Now!"

Susie scurries away with a last sympathetic glance towards her distressed patient.

Matthews is beside the patient in an instant, leaning over her and speaking in an urgent whisper. "Listen, I know you think I don't understand, but I do. My family shares your beliefs, but when my father needed an urgent transfusion we decided to choose life. Nobody has to know. We didn't tell the congregation and he's alive and well today. It's your choice – even your husband doesn't need to know if you don't want us to tell him."

Mrs Saunders is no longer sobbing. Her eyes are wide, her breaths short and she's looking at Matthews in astonishment.

Niklaus strides over to the pregnant woman's side takes hold of her arm lightly and whispers something in her ear. In this moment the woman's face goes blank and she stares off into the distance. After Niklaus releases his grasp, she picks up the pen and scribbles on the consent form without really looking at it. As she hands it back to Matthews she murmurs, "I don't want my baby to die. Please do everything you can to save both of us. Try to avoid giving us blood, but I understand if you have to. Leave it to me to tell my husband. Or not." Niklaus leaves her bedside and comes to stand by me again.

Matthews grabs the clipboard and flings aside the curtains then she heads to the nurses' station. I follow her with Niklaus on my heels. Matthews snatches the consent form from under the clip and summons Susie to her side. "I'll arrange an operating room as soon as possible. Run some blood work on Mrs Saunders and mark it critically urgent. I want to get this surgery done as fast as possible, she's bleeding internally and I don't want her to change her mind at the last second about the surgery." The nurse nods her head and turns to leave. Matthews stops her at the last second and leans towards her ear.

"Also, put Mrs Saunders on suicide watch after the surgery, and arrange a councillor to go and see her after she wakes up."

Susie looks up in surprise. "Is that really necessary?"

"Yes, and we need to be mindful of confidentiality. She's risking being cast out of her religious community if they find out she's accepted blood. For some people, it's worse to be the living dead than dying a martyr for your beliefs."

Niklaus takes my hand and leads me down the corridor towards the lift. He pushes through the veil and presses the up button. The doors open and we enter. Niklaus inputs a floor and we begin our ascent.

I look up at him and see him in a new light. "So, you do try to save lives occasionally."

"Very occasionally. It's not something that is my choice, it is more of an order from those above me. Like I said, it doesn't matter if the woman dies, only that the baby shall live."

We exit the lift on the maternity ward, and I'm surprised to see that the sun is up and it's late afternoon. It takes a second for my eyes to adjust.

"Why? What's going to happen in the future?"

Niklaus is walking ahead of me towards the large window that displays all the newborn babies. He pauses and holds out his hand towards me and I take it instinctively.

"Come on," he says, "I want to show you." He leads me through the window in between the cribs till we come to a humidicrib holding a tiny baby. The nameplate reads 'baby of Mrs Julie Saunders'. Niklaus puts his hand through the plastic and rests on the baby's arm.

"Touch him, and I'll try to show you what I see."

I push my hand through the plastic humidicrib and touch the soft, warm skin of the baby.

"Now close your eyes and focus on the baby," Niklaus says as he places his hand on my cheek, perhaps in an attempt to transfer his power to me.

I close my eyes and feel the warmth of his touch. I hear the sound of distant cheering and through the mists of my mind I see an enormous crowd. I sense they are all here to see the baby, except that he's a grown man now, and he's at the centre of it all. Tall and dark with wavy hair and the look of victory beaming on his face pumps his fist high from behind a podium. An older version of Julie Saunders is sitting near him, clapping with tears of joy on her beaming face. As suddenly as it appears, the vision is gone.

"Did you see?" Niklaus peers at me intensely.

"I saw a big crowd, and a podium."

"Is that all? That was only the beginning. That's what's going to happen now the baby has been born. You didn't see the alternative?"

"No, just the crowd and Mrs Saunders looking at her son."

"In my vision the baby grows into a man who becomes a politician. He prevents a great war that would have caused an atomic catastrophe if it were to go ahead. Instead of tearing apart each country, he will unify them all under one centralised government. You only saw his election victory."

"Why can't I see all that?"

"Probably because you're not like me. You're in my domain, my plane of existence, so you must be absorbing some of my power. But you're not one of us – you were human."

"Us?"

Niklaus, perhaps realising his debt to me for the brief intimacy we shared together has been paid, withdraws into his usual cool demeanour.

"Yes, there are others like me."

"What about others like me?"

Niklaus sweeps his hand through his hair. He draws me close and kisses me lightly. "No. There's nobody like you." And he vanishes.

CHAPTER 27

I am standing in Emergency, lingering around the nurses' station while watching Reeves from across the room. He is tending the arm of a young woman who is staring off into the distance. The long straight line that had cut deep into her forearm was testing the meticulous precision of Reeves' sewing skills as he stitches the flesh back together. Her mother and brother stand to one side of the bed, just beyond the curtain. Neither is paying much attention to the girl. The mother has an orderly and a security guard on either side of her and she keeps looking from one to the other and glancing towards her son while throwing erratic outbursts at him. The brother offers placatory words towards his mother and concerned glances towards his sister. He could only be in his mid-twenties, but seems years older, either from exhaustion or the early onset of responsibility. He's tall and scrawny with dishevelled hair that looks as though it hasn't been washed in a week or so.

Nicole strides across the ward, her eyes scanning around her. She spots the security guard then heads towards Susie who's sitting behind the desk. Susie looks up from her notes and they huddle together. I move closer to hear what they're whispering about. Susie always seems to know what's going on in the hospital, so maybe I'll get an update on Nicole and Reeves. I like Susie – she's a bubbly person and everyone finds her easy to talk to, but I don't know why they confide in her, as she can't keep any private information to herself.

"I heard the call to security from the break room. What's going on, Susie?"

Susie's eyes light up with the excitement of imparting news. "Remember that woman who was admitted last month?"

"The one we had to keep sedating to keep her from abusing staff?"

"The very same. She's back. Cast your eyes leftwards."

"Uh huh."

"Except this time it's her daughter who's here – suicide attempt – but the mum thinks it's a ruse to get her sectioned again."

"Pretty drastic ruse. Poor kid. First attempt?"

"Second. Swallowed a bunch of pills last time. Her brother found her slumped in front of the television..."

I don't want to hear anymore, I get the gist. I wander over to Marie's bedside to hear the conversation between Marie and Reeves.

"Why did you do this to yourself, Marie?"

"I just want it to be over. I don't want to keep on living."

Reeves seems momentarily perplexed by her tone. Marie's voice is mechanical, perfunctory.

"What can we do to help you?"

"Please, just let me die. I can't be around her anymore. I'm done."

Reeves looks up at Marie's mother.

"What the fuck are you looking at me for?" The older woman hisses at him through clenched teeth.

Reeves turns his attention back to the girl.

"I can't do that, I'm sorry. But we can get you help for the way you're feeling right now."

"I don't want help. I just want to die."

I become curious. Perhaps Marie's soul is cracked, like the souls of Albert or the heroin addict? I touch my hand to her chest and begin to pull, I get little resistance from her body and I see a light blue aurora at the end of my hands. It is not cracked and has no gashes over it, but I can feel its hurt and longing to be back on the other side. I can help this girl. I could release her soul and she could pass on peacefully. I look down at Marie's wrist and see that blood is seeping to the surface of the bandage. Reeves hasn't noticed and I doubt Marie will tell him, she genuinely wants to die. I wish I could see into her past like Niklaus can, see what has caused her so much pain in her life that makes her want to end it all.

I let go with my hands and her soul seeps back into her body, like the ebb of a wave being drawn back to the ocean. I hold her forearm above where the bandage is bound. I close my eyes and concentrate like I did with the small baby, but on that occasion I had Niklaus's help to guide me. Reeves is talking tentatively to Marie about treatment options and a likely stay in the psychiatric ward for a period until she's no longer a risk to herself. She doesn't look like she's listening. I block him out and try to tune in to Marie's soul. I must know whether her passing on would help her be at peace.

A small flash of light blinds my inner eye briefly before an image comes to me. A small kitchen where the benches are piled high with dirty plates and saucepans. Marie's mother snatches a filthy carving knife from the sink and swipes it through the air, keeping Marie and her brother away from her, telling the two of them to keep back else she'll hurt them.

The brother raises his hands with his palms outwards and his voice is soothing. "Mum, put down the knife. We're here to help you."

"No, you're not! You want to drug me and have me taken away. I won't let you do it! I'm fine the way I am."

"No mum you're not. You've stopped taking your medication again. This isn't you." The brother's voice is soft and reassuring.

The mother looks confused.

"No! The voices are telling me no! They help me. They don't keep secrets like you both do."

The brother edges forward then grabs the mother's wrist and raises it high above their heads. He wrestles the knife from her hand and flings it to the other side of the room.

"I told you to lock up all the sharps, Marie! You had one job to do!"

The brother's strong arms embrace and contain his mother. Marie scrambles after the knife.

The scene vanishes into black. I can't see anything this time but I can hear voices.

"Her mumma is crazy you know, that's why she's always filthy. Can't do nothing for herself."

"That brother of hers is supposed to be her guardian, you'd think he'd take better care of his sister instead of wasting his time trying to care for his mum. Should of just given her over to the state."

Everything goes quiet and as my eyes adjust to the dark I can see that Marie is asleep in bed. She is awoken by her mother pouncing on top of her and grabbing at her hair.

"I know you're a whore! You've been going out with those young boys, selling yourself."

"No mum, I haven't! What are you talking about? You're hurting me!"

"The voices! The voices told me I was bringing up a whore. That God will punish you for being so defiant."

Marie's mother yanks at her hair while Marie screams out for her brother.

"Anthony! Anthony, help!"

Anthony comes in and tackles his mother and pulls her off Marie. "This has got to stop Mum! We'll send you away if we have to! You gotta take your medication!"

Everything fades to black and I let go of Marie's wrist. I know I haven't seen the worst of it. I only caught a glimpse of what it was like to live as Marie. I want to help her; I can make all the pain she's experienced in her life dissolve and she can pass on, hopefully to live a better life next time around.

Reeves is still speaking to her about treatments but Marie looks disconnected. She has already made up her mind. The orderly comes to transport Marie to the psychiatric ward for observation. I don't follow the orderly. Instead I stay with Dr Reeves till he departs to get the file for his next patient.

I'm sitting in the doctors' mess watching TV. I try to concentrate on what is playing but I can't focus, so time begins to slip away from me. Reeves bursts through the door and rushes into the bathroom, his breath in gasps and his face distraught. I'm jolted back to reality and follow him. Reeves is sitting on the bench with his head in his hands, sobbing. I don't know what's happened but I suspect it has something to do with Marie. I sit beside Reeves and put my hand on his knee. I concentrate like I did before and I see an image of Marie lying slumped in a bathroom – bandages bloody and removed from around her wrists. Her complexion is pale and waxy and a bloody pen is beside her. She must have used the pen to rip away at the stitches that Reeves had put in place and has bled out on the floor of the hospital bathroom. She had finally achieved her desire.

I want to kiss away the tears that are glistening on his cheeks and hold him till he feels better. I rise off the bench and then kneel between Reeves' legs, peering up into his confounded face. I clutch his hand but I don't push through the veil – I want him to know I'm here for him but I don't want to startle him. I place a kiss on his hand then upon his wet cheek. I've noticed he is more attentive to his patients' emotional needs than some of the other doctors who seem to be able to compartmentalise their feelings towards their patients. I find it endearing but I think it takes a lot out of him.

The door behind us opens and Drac's assistant, Justin, strides in. Reeves brushes away his tears and straightens up.

"Wassup?" Justin says it automatically as he moves to the basin and turns on the tap, only glancing at Reeves.

"Hey Justin, not much. You?"

Something in Reeves' voice causes Justin to peer at him as he answers. "Nothin'. On break for a couple more minutes." Justin dries his hand on some paper towel and throws it in the bin. "You're not going soft on me are ya Reeves?"

"No, not at all."

"Cause this kinda work can break ya if ya don't rein in them feelings. Don't wanna end up like ya daddy, do ya?"

"I just had a hard day. A patient of mine killed herself upstairs in psych. She was so young…"

"Oh yeah, heard about that. Real shame, Reeves."

I lean forward and touch my hand to Reeves's cheek, even though I know he can't feel me. Reeves hauls himself up off the bench, walks through me and snatches a sheet of hand towel and blows his nose then heads towards the door. Justin holds the door open for Reeves then follows him out.

I turn around to trail after them but find Niklaus leaning on a cubicle door with his arms crossed.

"What were you doing?" His face is neutral but there's petulance in his voice.

"Nothing."

"You know you can't comfort him from this plane of existence."

"I know. I was just…"

Niklaus interjects. "Are you in love with him?"

"No, of course not," my voice is indignant but I can't look him in the eye.

"You have never been as tender with me."

"An opportunity hasn't presented itself when I would need to be."

Niklaus pushes himself off the cubicle door and moves towards me. I reach towards him and put my hand on his cheek. His body stiffens and his eyes are hostile. I've made good progress lately and been rewarded with information – I don't want to lose what I've gained because of his jealousy. I lean up and lightly brush my lips against his unresponsive lips. I move my hand from his porcelain cheek and run it lightly down his neck. Still he doesn't respond, but his hostility seems to be softening. I bring my lips to his ear and know he'll feel the warm breath of my voice on his skin.

"Why would I bother with a mortal boy when I have an immortal man who's never far away?" I flick my tongue across his top lip then pull away for a moment before repeating the action. This time he grabs the back of my head with his hands and possesses my mouth with his own, drawing me into a deep kiss. I wrap my arms around his neck and feel one of his arms slide around my waist and pull me close. I can tell his attention has been diverted away from Reeves and I feel a sense of empowerment being able to manipulate him in such a way. I can't help but wonder if I had this level of control over him when we first met.

Niklaus pulls away from my lips, which makes me think he might be withdrawing, until I feel his mouth launch at my throat and I feel his teeth grazing the side of my neck and his warm mouth nibbling my skin. I emit a squeal of surprise followed by a breathy giggle as tingles rush down my spine. I give in to the sensations and feel my neck stretching back so that my hair is flowing loosely past my shoulders.

"I want to touch you." Niklaus's voice booms into my ear and pulls me from reverie.

"What?"

"You heard me."

He pushes my trench coat off my shoulders and it drops to the floor.

"I want to feel your skin against my own." He pushes the straps of my black singlet off my shoulders and begins kissing the exposed flesh. I feel conflicted – uncertain of who's in control now. I long for him to sink his teeth into the flesh of my shoulders, but I feel I'm betraying Reeves. While my mind is contemplating the situation, my hand betrays me and creeps up his neck and my recalcitrant fingers glide through his dark hair. I feel like my body is making the decision for me as the echo of my former self takes over and I'm almost a bystander watching an event I'm powerless to control.

Niklaus stops for a moment and I feel suddenly afraid he's going to abandon me, but he pushes me up against a wall. He rips down my singlet straps and exposes my breasts – his firm hand grasps my breast and begins kneading the mound. His mouth captures mine again in a savage kiss. Using his index finger and thumb he rolls my nipple into a hard nub, causing my head to fling back into the tiled wall. I hear myself moan and I'm not sure if it's from pleasure or pain.

"Ava," he says as he cups my face in his hands and kisses my cheek. "Even after all this time you're still so perfect."

I grin like a fool hearing those words and giggle to myself at the absurdity of the situation. Being ravished by Niklaus in the doctors' bathroom – hardly a romantic setting. I can feel the wetness between my thighs and my clit begging to be fondled the same way he's fondling my breasts.

"Niklaus…"

He pauses, drops his hands to his sides and takes a small step back. "Sorry, did I…?"

"No, no… it's not you. It's well…" I indicate to our surroundings then lift my straps over my shoulders to cover my exposed breasts. I grab my trench coat from the floor then take Niklaus's hand. I lead him next door into the on-call room. I throw my trench coat onto a bed, then while facing Niklaus and looking directly into his eyes I peel down the straps of my singlet. My hair is draped across the front of my chest so I sweep it up and flick it behind my shoulders, arching my back instinctively to show off my full breasts. Niklaus turns towards the door, and for a terrifying moment I'm afraid he's about to leave, but he pushes through the veil and locks it. I walk up behind him and press my naked chest against him while running my hands under his arms and over his chest. I turn him around and push him against the wall. I kiss him again while my fingers flick open the black buttons of his collared shirt. I expose his chest and press myself against him. I feel a bulge swell in his pants and hear his breath increase. Niklaus deepens his kisses and runs his hand up my naked back into the ends of my hair. He grabs a chunk of hair and yanks it gently so my head is forced back and he has access to my neck. My hands delve down to the front of his pants to feel the firmness of his thighs as he sucks my neck near the base like a ravenous vampire. I moan slightly as I feel slight pain from the blood flushing the surface of my skin where he's sucking. I can resist temptation no longer and brush my hand over his thick hard cock. I rub him through his clothing and he releases the suction on my neck only to moan lightly in my ear and reciprocate by capturing my breast in one hand then leaning down and beginning to suckle on the adjacent nipple.

"Oh my god, Niklaus." I moan as I feel the tingling sensation in my nipple travel directly to my clit, causing a surge of wetness as he flicks his tongue on one nipple and teases the other with his thumb and forefinger. My cheeks feel flushed and my skin is on fire. I pull away from Niklaus to catch my breath and he looks up at me grinning.

"Good to see some things never change." He smiles and pecks my lips lightly. I grab his belt and lead him to an empty bed. I sit on the bed and undo Niklaus's belt while looking up at his smiling face. He brushes my cheek with his hand and I lean my face into his hand and kiss his palm. He shrugs his trench coat off his shoulders then peels off his open shirt. My eyes take in his naked torso – his body is beautifully toned and masculine. I look back up into his eyes and can tell he's basking in the pleasure of my gaze. He offers his hands and pulls me up to stand in front of him. His hands shift to my hips then he manoeuvres me so that I'm facing the bed and he sits on it before me. He undoes my button and the zipper of my jeans.

"Remember I said I want to touch you. I want to drive you mad with desire and exhilaration," he whispers in my ear.

Niklaus's lips are travelling across my stomach towards my

navel, sending little tingles that radiate to my clit. Niklaus's hands move over my hips to slide down my jeans and underwear. His kisses continue over my hip bone and to the boundaries of my pubic hair. His hands move over my skin then reach for mine to steady me as I step out of my clothing. Niklaus guides me onto his lap, and as I straddle him I'm delighted by the sensation of my skin against his. Niklaus looks calm and confident while I feel flushed and slightly embarrassed to be naked and exposed in front of him. My heart is pounding in my chest and my groin is heavy with desire as Niklaus's hands move over my thighs and hips, then up my back. He pulls me close so that my breasts are pressed up against his chest. As Niklaus sweeps my hair off my breasts and pushes it back over my shoulders, I catch his eyes for a moment and see a glimpse of concern.

"What is it? What's the matter?"

Niklaus grimaces for a second then relaxes. His words are delivered slowly and with intense concentration. "We don't have to continue if you don't want to do."

I feel a surge of affection for him in this moment. I've never seen him so conflicted before. His tremendous containment of his own desires in consideration of my feelings makes me stop for a moment and question my motives.

"I don't know whether I'm ready to... it's been so long, I feel outside of myself..."

As I trail off I see the disappointed look in his eyes, but he composes himself.

"It's alright. We don't have to—"

"But you want to?" I interject with a sudden fear that he has given up too easily.

"Of course! I want to possess you completely, but only if you want me as much as I want you." Niklaus trails his finger softly down my chest. "Besides, there are other things we can do. I want to give you pleasure."

Niklaus squeezes my erect nipple and my breath catches as his hot mouth captures the adjacent nipple. I moan as his tongue flicks and circles the little erect nub. I pull away from him so his mouth is plucked from my breast. He looks up at me with his dark eyes and I kiss him deeply. His hand explores my thigh and slides up to my hip then my stomach. His palm descends to my pubic bone, lingering in my dark pubic hair. My breathing increases and my anticipation begins to mount. The tips of his fingers caress my outer lips as his middle finger glides over my clitoris and slips inside me. I know I'm slick, hot and wet, and I don't feel embarrassed. It's so exhilarating to feel him penetrating me, pushing inside and out until my hips move rhythmically to meet his thrusts. Just when I feel I can stand it no longer he withdraws his finger and it circles my aching clit. I moan encouragement into Niklaus's ear and hold him closer. My stomach is filled with butterflies and my heart is pounding. Niklaus applies a little more pressure and an additional finger so my slippery clit is completely encompassed by his nimble digits. I dig my nails into his shoulder as I feel something building in my core, the hum of electricity is mounting gradually. I'm breathing heavily into Niklaus's ear and a little flash of a memory reminds me that he likes his ears being played with. I stretch out my tongue and suckle and nibble his earlobes and am rewarded with a deep groan from Niklaus as his hand slides down so his fingers can penetrate my opening. The feeling of his fingers inside me while his palm is grinding into my clit causes the electricity to surge through my body into my brain. I'm on the brink and I call out.

"Niklaus, don't stop! Please don't stop, I'm so close."

"That's good my darling." Niklaus's voice is partway between a growl and a whisper. "I want you to explode for me."

Given an order like that causes me to fall off the side of the world, consumed with pleasure I moan loudly and my hips gyrate in rhythm with Niklaus's hand. I throw my head back in ecstasy and let out an unencumbered primal scream, safe in the knowledge that no earthly being can hear it. My vision goes black for a second as my body and senses drift into oblivion. I force my eyelids to open and focus on him as I reach up to Niklaus's face and run my hands down his cheek. He returns my gaze as he lifts his fingers up to his mouth and slides each one in slowly. His smile is mischievous and knowing.

"You still taste the same."

He kisses me again this time placing his other hand in my hair, scrunching it up and holding it tight. I feel greedy and want more. My hands move from Niklaus's shoulders to his belt and my fingers fumble with the buckle.

"I thought you said you didn't want to..."

"I don't. Shh!"

I crawl off him and pull him by his trousers, forcing him to stand. I remove them but leave his underwear in place. His cock is strained against the confines of his black boxer briefs. Funny how everything that comes through the veil is black – even his underwear. I resist sharing this observation with him. I put my palm against his engorged cock and rub firmly. Niklaus groans and wraps his arms around my neck, meeting my forehead with his. Our faces are close enough to feel each other's breath.

"You have no idea how long I've wanted you to touch me like this." Niklaus whispers then kisses my forehead, my temple, my cheek. He holds me close while my hands grasp his cock.

I let go of his bulging cock and push him backwards so that the back of his knees buckle against the frame of the metal bed and he plonks down with a grating squeak. I lean forward and place one knee on the mattress then stretch the other across his hip then straddle him again. I crave the feeling of our naked skin touching, but I resist the temptation, enjoying hovering above him and watching the desire in his eyes rise to a screaming pitch. I'm delirious with delight at seeing Niklaus's ethereal composure slipping away. After a moment I can hold back no longer – my skin craves the sensation of his skin on mine – I glide closer to his body and feel a frisson surge through mine. Niklaus puts his hand behind my neck and pulls me close to kiss me again. His hands are exploring my body and I know I must feel feverish. My body is on fire and my clit is pulsing. Begging for more. This time I want Niklaus to feel satisfaction. My hands go through his dark hair and I pull at the roots of his scalp while my hips grind against him. Our genitals are separated only the thin film of his black under-garments and the feeling is intoxifying. My throbbing clit has found his hard cock and I press myself against him so I can appease the pulses and feel the electricity radiate through-out my groin into my core. Niklaus groans as I rock and grind against him.

"Yes, just like that." He grabs the flesh of my naked arse and squeezes hard, pushing and pulling with my rhythm.

"Does that feel good?" I ask Niklaus as I slow down and work the length of his cock from base to tip.

"Yes. Keep going. I like the way you feel."

"Do you want me to come all over your cock?" My voice is a husky whisper but I feel powerful. I can only imagine what he'd do if I stopped right now and left him unsatisfied.

"Yes, my love. I want you to let go for me, and only for me, for eternity."

I can feel the electricity building once again and I'm con-sumed with the thought of being Niklaus's captive for an eternity. The old Avaline, couldn't be more delighted. This was her girlish dream. The new me can hardly bear the thought – I want to be free. I want to be out of here and on the other side where I belong. These thoughts are getting in the way of my orgasm.

"What's the matter?" Niklaus looks at my face with concern.

"Nothing," I mutter. I'm surprised that he's so aware to my every nuance. I hadn't realised my thoughts betrayed me. I can see no option available to me other than to fake it. I clutch Niklaus tightly and heave my breasts then I take a deep breath and let out a loud moan. I glimpse at Niklaus who looks pleased. He pulls me close and watches my face as I theatrically 'orgasm'. Niklaus kisses me over and over again like he's hungry for me and nothing other than me will grat-ify him. He holds me by the waist and rolls on top of me. My lust is beginning to fade but I can still feel Niklaus's hard cock still pressed against my vulva. Niklaus rests on his elbows and looks down at me. His eyes have softened, there's a twitch of a smile around his lips and I've never seen him look so vulnerable. I'm reminded of Waterhouse's painting of the soldier looking down at Lamia. I lift my hand and stroke his cheek with my index and middle finger. I'm surprised I haven't noticed before how handsome he is – his cheekbones look like they've been carved by Michelangelo and his nose is strong, straight and masculine. I lean up and kiss him delicately then wrap my arms around him and pull him close to me. Niklaus buries his face in my hair that is splayed across the pillow. I feel sad and I don't know why. Is it because I can never leave? Or because one day I will? I don't know how I know this, but I'm certain my existence can't continue indefinitely here in Niklaus's domain. I fleetingly recall Albert's promise to me, but quickly squash the thought down, not daring to hope he'll ever succeed.

Niklaus rolls off me but still clutches me close "You're all I ever wanted," he whispers to me. "I could have existed forever without any companionship. I had no need or want to be close to another but you changed all of that for me, Ava. You consume me."

I roll onto my side and look at Niklaus. He's resting his hand on my waist and our faces are close together. "I wish I could remember what it was like to be with you."

"You will," he whispers. "If you stay on this plane for long enough, memories will come back to you. You'll eventually remember all your previous lives in full and you'll want nothing more than to be here with me, like this."

"This is what she wanted, isn't it?" Niklaus grabs my hand and kisses my fingertips. "I can remember her desire to be immortal and to be with you forever. Being with you made her feel safe."

"How does it make you feel?" he asks me.

I think for a moment then reply. "Conflicted." I pull my hand away from his lips. "Part of me remembers loving you, but I think I'm only with you now because I'm alone."

I see this visibly stings Niklaus; he shuts his eyes, swallows hard and pulls me close so my skin is pressed against his. He kisses my forehead and says "It won't always be like this. You'll learn to love me again. You'll remember everything."

Part of me knows he's right. It may take a long time but eventually everything will piece together and the feelings I had for him will flood back.

The doorknob jiggles and then there's a knock. After a beat the knock happens again "Is there anybody in there? Can someone let me in?"

Silence.

Muffled voices can be heard through the door. "Sometimes the door locks on itself from the inside."

"I'll go get maintenance."

"That sounds like our cue to get dressed," I say.

"Why?" Niklaus pulls me closer. "They can't see us. We can stay like this."

"Yeah well, I'd rather not be naked when they enter." I push him away, sit up and lean over the edge of the bed to collect my underwear and singlet. I feel Niklaus's hand on my back, followed by his lips.

"Your back was always my favourite area of your body. The skin there is so soft and silken to the touch. It used to put you in the mood when I kissed your shoulders and up your neck." Niklaus sits up and kisses my shoulder I pull away.

"I've had enough, I don't want to get caught."

"Ava, it is physically impossible for us to get caught. Come back to bed."

"No!" I pull on my dark jeans and stand fully dressed.

Niklaus sighs then pulls his legs over the edge of the bed, he collects his pants and pulls them on. Gathering the rest of his clothing items he stands up.

"Fine, but I'll be back soon and I'll be hoping for a repeat performance." He smirks and kisses me briefly before dissipating.

I pick up my trench coat off the adjacent bed and shrug it over my shoulders. I leave the room as the maintenance man opens the door.

CHAPTER 28

Hot mist runs down my back. I am naked in the shower after being with Niklaus. Even though I can't really feel the heat of the water, I need time to relax and reflect. Only one thing comes to my mind while I'm showering. Elwood. My body is primed and ready, I feel sexual, powerful and liberated for the first time in decades. Feeling like this reminds me of being with Elwood. If I concentrate I can remember him: Tanned skin, even though the sun rarely peeked through the smog in London during the war; a lean body, thanks to rationing. He was muscular but didn't work out. He had side-skirted military service because he was needed in London, and because his affluent wife had pulled a few strings keeping him from going abroad. Elwood was always clean shaven and smelt nice no matter what time of the day or night it was. His confidence and charisma knew exactly how to keep a girl spellbound. When he used to stride past the nurses' station I would bite my knuckles so hard it would leave an indentation. I remember momentary flirtations, brushing against him on purpose and whispering suggestively into his ear just to watch him get riled. When he used to kiss me it was electric, tingles used to go down my spine to my core. His touch made me bite my lip and throw my head back in ecstasy. I remember being pushed against a wall, while hands groped my thighs, seeking my suspender hooks and unfastening them one at a time then removing the rationed stockings with sweet kisses down my legs.

I rub my hands over my face wiping away the droplets that have accumulated on my face. It occurs to me that Niklaus was probably present for at least some of my escapades while I was alive. He said he was always watching over me, more so during the war, so he must have seen me with Elwood. I feel a pang of guilt. Seeing me with another man would have been hard for him when he loves me unconditionally. I wonder briefly whether it bothered him. My guilt worsens. Why though? I owe Niklaus nothing. I remain here in his domain, not out of choice. It would have been Avaline's choice, if she had been given the option.

Shut up! I am not her!

I was her. Past tense. I shake my head. I was her a long time ago, not now. I am my own woman, making my own decisions. I am free to choose whoever I want and I choose Elwood.

Jason!

I choose Jason, if given the choice.

I sit on the tiled floor under the cascading waters and sink my face into my hands. I can't even remember what sex feels like. My brain disagrees and I get a quick flash of being with Elwood in the on-call room, naked between the sheets, giggling and begging to be released from his grip.

I feel demented. Torn between my past lives, and these are the only two that are surfacing. I suspect this is because of Niklaus's impact on both of them.

CHAPTER 29

I don't think I can spend eternity here in this hospital – reaping souls and following nurses. What would happen if the hospital were to close? Would I be locked in here wandering the empty corridors forever? What happens when the building gets torn down to make way for something new? Will I be released from the confines of these grounds? That seems like a long time to wait to find out. Perhaps if I don't pay attention time will escape my grasp and I'll find out sooner? Like going to sleep and waking at the end of a movie. I suppose that would be giving up – am I ready to give up? While contemplating these thoughts I follow Margie as she goes down a corridor towards the nurses' station in Emergency. Susie is there as always, and greets Margie with an excited smile.

"You'll never guess who was admitted last night!"

"Who?" Margie smiles in response.

"Harold Barden!" Susie's voice lowers to a conspiratorial hush. "That man who was being trialled as a child killer all those years ago. The one who was acquitted because the evidence was tampered with. He came in with some heart difficulties last night and they're keeping him here under observation."

I've been around long enough to know when Margie feels uncomfortable. Her expression doesn't change much but there's a tightness around her mouth and a twitch between her eyes.

"Are you alright Marg?" Susie asks.

"Fine." Margie plasters a fake smile across her face as she collects some patient files and looks them over. "Will he be here for long?"

"No, I expect that they'll release him tomorrow."

"Where is he?"

"Cardiology. He has angina, I think. At least that's what they're saying upstairs."

Margie nods and looks as though she's making friendly banter, but I'm not convinced.

I follow Margie as she makes her rounds and attends to patients. It's her break time but she isn't heading for the break room behind the nurses' station. Margie takes the lift to the cardiology department, so I trail after her. She shuffles down the hallway to Barden's room and slips in through the open door.

She closes it behind her and presses her body against the door. That doesn't stop me, I just push through the wall.

"Do you remember Kieran Dobson?" Margie asks.

Barden remains silent while looking towards her.

Margie pushes off the door and takes a few slow steps towards the bed. "Good kid. He used to live next door to me and my husband. He hanged himself when he was 15."

Barden's eyes haven't shifted from Margie. His voice is even and controlled. "I'm sorry to hear that."

"You should be sorry. In his note he mentions you."

Barden's expression hasn't changed, but there's an intensity to his voice. "What do you want from me?"

"I want you to pay for what you've done, not just to the people who came forward, but for the people who didn't."

"What are you going to do about it? Report me?"

Suddenly I can see Margie though Barden's eyes. I've been with her so long I sometimes forget she's an unfit woman in her sixties.

Margie stays silent and doesn't move. She looks Barden in the eye and doesn't back down.

"That's what I thought. Nothing. There's nothing you can do." Barden's voice is taunting and confident.

"When there are predators like you in the world, I'm glad I don't have children."

"Don't? Or can't? Left it a bit late now, haven't you, Love?"

Margie glares at him as her nostrils flare and her chest heaves. She turns abruptly and leaves the room.

I stay with Margie for the rest of the day, partly out of concern, but mostly in case something interesting happens. She seems agitated and distracted.

It's the end of Margie's shift but instead of going home she's heading for the cardiology ward again. It's late in the night and most of the patients are sleeping. Margie enters Barden's room and I trail in behind her. His eyes are closed, his mouth is slightly open and his breaths are deep and audible. She doesn't turn on the light but instead manoeuvres the room by feel. Margie pulls a syringe from her pocket and draws up air then locks the syringe into the IV port. She stands there for a long moment doing nothing. I watch mesmerised. I don't think she can do it. As much as Margie hates this man and wants balance in the universe by Barden meeting his death, she can't bring herself to be the one to take it. Margie takes a few breaths and is murmuring something under her breath that I can't hear. She's trying to psych herself into pushing the plunger. Barden stirs in his sleep and she freezes, holding her breath. Barden settles again. Margie withdraws the syringe and ejects the air. She replaces it in her pocket and leaves. I look down at Barden sleeping peacefully, in spite of all the crimes he's committed and the lives he's tormented by his existence. I'm tempted to plunge my hand deep to his chest and rip out his soul. I'd do it for Margie and for his victims, to give them justice when the world has offered them none.

I can feel hands on my shoulders and a chaste kiss upon my

cheek. I turn around and see Niklaus standing before me. He leans in and kisses me on the lips. I feel a sense of warmth and familiarity that surprises me and stops me pulling away from him.

"What are you doing?" he asks me.

"Nothing," I say as I turn and look down at Barden lying in the hospital bed. Niklaus turns my face back towards him and leans down and kisses me deeply. I pull away from the intensity of the embrace and look up at him. "Do you want to go for a walk?"

Niklaus nods and we walk out of the room together, heading towards the hospital gardens. Niklaus doesn't take my hand or put his arm around me, but I sense he seems content with just being beside me.

"How are you feeling since we…?" Niklaus's voice trails off.

My eyebrows arch in surprise. I'm surprised that Niklaus cares how I feel about our intimate liaison.

"I'm fine." My mind flashes back to our passionate exchange and I feel the edge of my mouth twitch. "It was nice."

Niklaus beams. "I think so too. I was afraid you might be feeling remorseful and that maybe you wouldn't want to do it again."

"Oh." I hadn't really considered being intimate with Niklaus again. To be honest I hadn't though much of the situation at all. It seems like it was weeks ago and my mind has been distracted by the commotion of having a paedophile at the hospital. "I suppose we could. I can't think of a reason not to."

Niklaus's face lights up like a teenager on his first date. "Good! I was hoping you'd say that."

The rhythmic sound of our footsteps crunching along the pebble stone path is soothing. I've watched the seasons change this garden over so many years. In a flash I recall the war years and walking through this garden with Elwood when we were both employed here, although then it was fresh produce growing instead of flowers – a nod to the war effort. We used to take every chance to slip outside so we could talk freely, but always holding back from touching each other because of prying eyes from the hospital – a shadow always over us warning us that gossip might reach the ears of his wife.

"Niklaus, you said you were around a lot during the war. Did you ever see me with Elwood Reeves?"

Niklaus's nose wrinkles up like he's smelt something foul. "Mmm... I did."

"Did you ever watch us...?"

Niklaus interrupts me. "No, of course not!"

"Oh. Sorry, I just wondered."

"Why would I want to see you with another man?"

"It was just something that occurred to me and I thought I'd ask."

Niklaus shakes his head and lets out a sigh.

We sit on the bench in the stark winter garden, the bare stalks of the rose bushes glinting with frost. Niklaus stretches his legs out straight and his arms across the back of the bench. I exhale and my breath billows out of my mouth and lingers in the air. I feel a chill that cuts through my coat and flick my collar up around my neck and plunge my icy fingers into the pockets. If it's cold enough for me to notice, the weather beyond the veil must be sub-zero. I nudge a little closer to Niklaus for warmth and snuggle in under his arm. I know he won't mind.

"Are you cold?" Niklaus puts his arm around my shoulder.

"Mmm, a little."

Niklaus stands and slides off his coat. He places it over my shoulders then sits down and pulls me close to him.

"What about you? Aren't you cold now?"

Niklaus chuckles. "Well it's not like it'll kill me."

I laugh and look at him. His cheeks don't go rosy like mine do when I'm cold. He's different, unhuman. His features resemble a mortal man's, and sometime I forget he's not. He is Death. The only time he doesn't look like a marble statue is when he smiles or laughs, although this isn't a frequent occurrence.

Niklaus strokes my flushed cheek with the back of his hand; his extremities radiate warmth against my icy skin. He leans in and kisses me on my forehead. He pulls me close to him and I feel warm and safe from the frosty air. He rests his head on top on mine and inhales the scent of my hair.

"This is all I ever wanted. To be with you like this again."

"How long has it been since you were last with her?"

Niklaus is quiet for a moment, apart from a soft murmur that suggests he's either reluctant to answer, or is casting his mind back.

"We met in the mid-1700s. I can't remember the exact year. It was a long time ago."

I wait. Unsure as to whether to respond or wait until he offers me more information.

"Ava, I've grown extremely fond of you. While I understand that you're not Avaline, you're as kind, compassionate and as beautiful as she was. I've grown to love you as your own person, not just as a reflection of the past."

My body jerks forward on the bench. He pulls me back under his arm.

"You're in love with me?" I feel confused and my heart is pounding – fuelled by fight or flight hormones.

I hadn't considered that Niklaus's obsession for me could be counted as love, though in his mind he probably can't differentiate between the two.

"I've loved you for centuries, Ava. Although the love I have for you now is different to what it used to be. I don't expect you to understand, or feel the same way, but I'm glad you've grown more accustomed to us being intimate with each other."

I draw a breath to reply, but I can't think of anything to say to him, and my words become a cloud of vapour in front of my face. I hadn't considered my feelings towards Niklaus, beyond him being a welcome distraction from the endless monotony and isolation of my existence. A snowflake lands on Niklaus's cheek and rests there unmelting. I wipe it away from his skin with my index finger then lean in and kiss his pale lips. I feel I have to offer him something as I can't echo his sentiments. I place my hand on his cheek and deepen the kiss.

Niklaus returns my kiss then pulls away. "Ava, I still ache for you. When you kiss me like this my world crumbles before your feet. You've no idea the effect you have on me."

I smile and slide my hand from his cheek down to the bulge in his trousers. "I think I do, Niklaus."

He grabs my hand and shifts it to his knee and holds it there.

"I'm sorry, did I make you feel uncomfortable?"

I love it when Niklaus chuckles. It's a deep throaty sound and his eyes crinkle up. "No, not at all. You just took me by surprise. The old Avaline wouldn't have done that."

"I suppose there was a stronger sense of propriety back then."

I bite my lip and blush a deeper crimson. *Be brave, he'd never reject you.* I kiss him again and push my hand back to his crotch.

"Don't forget, when I was young there was a war on." I give him what I hope is a cheeky wink as I fondle his erect cock. He's told me that his body has been aching for mine for centuries. I stand and take a step back from him, bite my lip seductively. I look down to my jeans and undo the top button. Niklaus doesn't need any prompting. He stands and sweeps me into his arms as the garden shimmers into blackness around me. I feel before seeing we're back in the hospital because there's a rush of warmth around me that wafts around my cheeks and thaws my fingers. My eyes adjust and I see we're in a darkened corridor on the med surgical ward. Niklaus takes my hand and guides me to a vacant private room containing a single bed, nightstand and bedside chair. He doesn't turn on the light, but instead strips the bed by the light of the moon shining in through the window. He throws the blankets and pillows onto the carpeted floor, then turns to me and reaches out his hands.

"I want this...I want this with you, Niklaus." I shrug my coat off my shoulders and take a step towards him.

"Then you shall have me. You will always have me, Ava." Niklaus unbuttons his shirt and reveals his chiselled body beneath. My hand reaches out instinctively and moves over his body while my mouth swoops on his neck, leaving a trail of kisses from his nape up to the base of his ear. I graze my teeth over his ear lobe. Niklaus draws a sharp breath then he grabs my arse, fingers delving into my muscles. Niklaus grasps my shoulders and pushes me against the wall, wrapping his hand around my neck while he invades my mouth with his tongue. I nip his lip and he jerks his head back.

"You can't stand not being in control, can you Niklaus?"

Niklaus removes his hand from my neck and cups my breasts through the fabric of my singlet top. He teases my nipples with his thumb and forefingers. He bows his head and trickles kisses down my neck. "Hmmm... I find I can lose a little control around you. Death is not designed to be submissive."

"What's it like to be with you when you're out of control?" I ask as I loosen the belt of his jeans.

Niklaus cups my face in his hands and I gaze into his dark eyes. "It's not like this. It's not how I want to be with you."

He kisses me and pours his soul into me through his lips. I feel every pang of jealously he's ever felt, the depth of his loneliness through the centuries, and the feeling of wholeness he's experiencing now. Nothing makes me want to leave him in this moment. I wrap my arms around his neck and pull him closer to me so I can feel his organ pressing against my sex.

Niklaus slips his hands under my singlet top and we break our kiss just long enough for him to slip it over my head, revealing my full breasts. He pulls me by the waist away from the wall. My hands grapple with the zipper of my dark denim jeans. I lie back on the blankets and pillows on the floor and ease the tight material down my long, toned legs. I watch the expression on Niklaus's face as he gazes at my body in the semi-darkness. He kneels down in between my legs and glides his body over mine.

I'm surprised at how heavy he feels, because he looks so lean and has always seemed so ethereal to me. His weight is comforting and my arms instinctively reach around him. I want to feel his mouth on every inch of me, I want to be drowned in euphoria and never resurface. I trail my fingers down his back then wrench at his jeans and underwear. I have never desired anything more than to feel his naked skin against my own. Niklaus's body lifts off mine to give me room to remove his garments, and now the only thing that stands between us becoming one is my underwear which is damp with readiness for him. I clasp Niklaus's neck and raise my head so I can whisper in his ear.

"Please Niklaus, I've never needed you so badly." I feel his cock twitch at my opening. "I want to feel you inside me."

Niklaus groans then his lips are on me, teasing my nipples as I gasp with unexpected pleasure. His tongue laps at the tough nubs of my chest. I bite my lip and swallow hard as I let out a moan. I hadn't expected Niklaus to show so much restraint. He pulls my underwear down my thighs and I am overwhelmed with gratitude. Niklaus sits back on his heels looking me over greedily. My knee is bent and he had a hand on my outer thigh, he pushes the other knee out of the way, so as not to spoil the view. He runs his hand down my inner thigh, which sends shivers up through my sex into my core. *Is he going to make me beg?* My breath quickens and I try to look seductive. Niklaus grasps his cock in his hand, draws me closer then runs his cock up the length of my sex. I let out a loud moan when the head of his cock brushes against my clit.

"Oh you're so ready for me," Niklaus mutters as he inserts the tip of his cock into my vagina. My skin feels a wave of fire, my nerves stand on edge and I feel tortured.

"Niklaus, please. Isn't this exactly what you've wanted for centuries?"

Niklaus continues rocking the tip of his cock in and out of my opening. "Not exactly. All I've ever wanted was to be with you. Sex, while relevant, wasn't the ultimate goal."

I sit up on my elbows and peer into Niklaus's face. "What is relevant right now is how badly I want you, Niklaus. Nothing could tear me away from you right now." I push myself up, grab his shoulders and pull him towards me, locking my lips on his. Niklaus steadies himself with his arm outstretched. He falls gently on top of me, bracing himself on his forearms so as not to crush me. Without taking his eyes from mine he shifts his weight to his left arm and reaches down my body with his right. His free hand guides his member into my opening and fills me. He groans as my internal warmth devours his cock. I let out a grasp.

This is all I could ever want, to be one with him.

My own thoughts shock me, as if they're coming from somewhere deep within, or from some foreign corner of my mind I didn't know existed. Part of me registers these thoughts don't feel like mine but in this moment, I don't care. Nothing else matters. The world could fall down around us and I wouldn't notice because I am lost in oblivion with him.

Niklaus strokes my insides and I feel warm at my core, his cock stoking the fire within me. My hands move up onto his muscular back and I dig my nails deep into his flesh as my breathing hitches. Niklaus winces in pain and grabs my arms, I relinquish control of his back and I let him pin my wrists above my head. He buries his head in the nape of my neck among my hair. I gasp as I can feel my climax building. I draw up my knees so Niklaus can penetrate me deeply and so his cock can stroke my g-spot. As I moan in his ear, he lets go of my wrists and wraps his arms around under me, holding tight. I think he's as close as I am. The involuntary cry that's fighting for release explodes from deep within my lungs as my body arches and shudders against him until I'm finally spent. It's as if we've done this dance a thousand times as he instinctively knows he can give in to his primal urge. His breaths are short and fast as his thrusting quickens for a few strokes then he hovers over me for a moment, a soft sigh exhaling from him the only indication it's over.

I open my eyes as Niklaus leans on his elbows and looks down at me with a smile, his fingers twirling a long strand of my hair. I place my hands on his back and can feel the thin film of sweat on his skin. I close my eyes and smile to myself, enjoying the endorphins throbbing away in my veins. Niklaus kisses my forehead then withdraws himself from me and moves to my side. As I roll towards him the strand of hair Niklaus was playing with obscures my view of him. Niklaus sweeps the lock from my face and tucks it behind my ear in a gesture that feels surprisingly intimate. The moonlight casts a soft light over our naked bodies, but I'm glad it's dim enough in the room to partly conceal my features as I suddenly feel exposed. Strange that I long for comfort from the entity that's making me feel so vulnerable. I reach out and take Niklaus's hand in mine, intertwining our fingers then press my lips against his knuckles.

Niklaus meets my forehead with his then tilts his chin and kisses my brow before wrapping his arm around my waist and pulling me so close that I'm nestled into his chest. We stay like this for hours in comfortable silence until the dawn peeks over horizon and sunlight filters into the room. Niklaus lets out a long sigh as he eases his arm from under me. "I have to go."

I raise myself up onto my elbows. "Hmm, why?"

"Because if I say much longer there will be too much imbalance in the universe."

"So people can't die unless you're there?"

"Sort of… not really. It's hard to explain"

"Do you think you'll ever explain it all to me one day?"

The corner of Niklaus's lip cracks into a smile. "Technically, I already have explained it all to you."

I dig Niklaus in the ribs. "Avaline doesn't count."

Niklaus's eyes crinkle and his mouth resists a grin as he rummages through the bedding for his clothes. As he pulls on his pants and shirt, I draw the blanket around my naked body. Standing above me, fully clothed and with his coat over his arm he leans down for a final kiss.

"I'll come back as soon as I can get away." He takes a step away then turns to look at me. "This is my new favourite memory of us." Then he vanishes.

I recover my jeans and tank top from the floor and pull them on. I examine the strewn bedding for signs of sexual activity but no fluids have crossed the veil. I remake the bed with tight hospital corners then leave the room to wander the corridors.

CHAPTER 30

I walk through the door and down the corridor towards the nurses' station, where I can see a bustle of people crowded around the counter. *Must be shift change.* As I get closer and hear the chatter of a dozen nurses sharing patient handover with each other. I compare the faces of the nurses to see who looks fatigued and ready to clock off, while also considering who might be interesting to follow this morning. I've been trailing after nurses for so long I know how the morning will progress. Obs, medications, breakfast, showers and bed linens changed. The character of the nurse is what will make my day interesting.

In the corner I spot Susie chattering with an older African nurse in green scrubs whose name I can't pronounce. Susie's hands are waving about as she retells the story of her children being afflicted with gastro on a recent road trip through France. The African nurse is standing with her arms crossed over her chest, she's smiling and nodding politely while her eyes dart back and forth at the clock on the wall.

As the last of the cohort drift away down the corridors or towards the main exit, Susie finishes up her story, scoops up the patient charts off the bench and strides down the hallway. I follow after Susie, glancing behind to see the relieved nurse toddle off towards the lockers so she can finally go home after being held captive by a woman as merciless as Niklaus. I lose sight of Susie as she turns a corner and before I catch up, Reeves comes barrelling towards me in his white coat, stethoscope flailing around his neck, hands clutching a patient file. It seems like a long time since I've seen him and I come to an abrupt halt. I'm directly in his path and I don't have time to skip to one side so his solid body passes through mine.

Ordinarily, I feel nothing when something passes through me, but this time it feels like bellyflopping onto stagnant water with a shard of glass piercing my heart.

As the sharp sensation eases it's replaced with a heavy sense of guilt. I've done nothing wrong so why am I feeling this way?

I have a perplexing impression that I've cheated on Reeves.

Immediately I set to work on justifying my actions to alleviate this useless emotion. I haven't got any kind of relationship with Jason. It's just a little crush. We've kissed only once and I'm the only one who can remember it. He doesn't even know I exist.

There must be a way to ease my conscience. I'm standing in the corridor with a heavy disturbing weight inside me. Do I keep following after Susie? Or switch around towards Reeves? I wish I could apologise to him; tell him that having sex with Niklaus meant nothing to me and that I don't feel anything for him other than hatred.

But is that true?

I reflect on my intimate exchange with Niklaus, and I can't work out whether it just happened or if it was days ago. In the moment with him I did feel something. I was in awe of his ethereal beauty, looking at him made my skin hot and my body craved to be close to his. I wanted to kiss him and I was thrilled with his devotion, which satiated a bone-deep itch. At the end of it all I wanted our skin touching and limbs intertwined – but were these thoughts and feelings my own? Or were they just a welcome distraction from the endless nightmare that is my existence?

Avaline's essence is buried somewhere within me. On this plane I can revisit my soul's memories – perhaps emotions have a way of seeping through as well? Could Avaline's echo be influencing my feelings for Niklaus?

Ting.

Saved by the bell. For once my call to duty is a pleasant distraction from my own internal conflict. I close my eyes and follow the bell.

CHAPTER 31

I swivel around and head back to the nurses' station, but instead of going towards one of the wards the ting draws me towards the stairs. I drift down a couple of flights and come out near the big sliding doors at the entrance to the hospital. I glance outside, but there are no ambulances waiting with new patients. The ting persists and I follow the sound down the driveway, across the trimmed front lawn to the edge of the hospital grounds. I walk towards the large iron gates that I've never seen closed and see a black sports car askew across the driveway. One tyre has mounted the gutter and the front bumper looks like it only just missed the ornate gates.

I hear a clear, loud ting. This must be it. As I approach the vehicle, the driver's door swings open and a dark suited leg flops out onto the ground, the shiny steel tip of black leather shoe clinking on the bitumen. The driver is well dressed and his shaven head is leaning back on the headrest as one hand clutches his abdomen. His breaths are quick and laboured. He seems to be struggling to remain conscious. His head rolls towards me and his squinting brown eyes lock on to mine.

"Are you going to help me or just vatch me bleed out?" His voice is guttural and there's an accent I can't quite place, but I'm reminded of a Chekov play I must have seen once.

The little bell in my head seems to indicate that even if I could help get him into the hospital, his chances of surviving his injuries would be slim.

"I'm sorry, I think it's too late."

The man breathes harder; I think it's in frustration but it's hard to tell.

"I can make it vorth your vile. I'm a vealthy and vell connected man."

"There's nothing you can offer me that will make any difference."

The man's looks down at his hand covering the wound. He shifts his hand to see the extent of the damage, and once with the pressure removed the wound begins to pulse dark red blood. The man's brow scrunches as he throws his head back onto the seat rest. Without looking at me he speaks again.

"Vhat's your name?"

"Ava."

"Well then Ava, if you don't help me inside and I do survive, I'll have you hunted down and left for dead, so you can understand how I feel right now."

I laugh out loud at the thought of being left for dead. I don't think the man has realised he's on the verge of death and is speaking to its personification. He's driving a luxury car and his suit looks tailor-made, so he could be a legitimate businessman. But his heavy gold jewellery, the oozing bullet wound and a large chest tattoo peeking out of the top of his white collared shirt hint at underworld connections.

"Drug deal gone wrong?" My curiosity is roused.

"No. It vas set up– to take me out."

The bell is getting louder, but I delay reaping his soul. This is more interesting than my monotonous existence. And is a distraction from my internal conflict.

"Who would want to do that?"

"I von't talk. Not to you. Get me inside!"

"Perhaps you'd prefer to talk to the police. Because that's what will happen if you go in there. They always call the police in for gunshot wounds." I throw my thumb in the direction of the hospital.

"Good."

Good? That seems to crush my gangster theory. His eyelids grow heavy and his head rolls back away from me. I sense he'll be ready to cross over soon.

"What's your name?"

"Viktor." His words are a drowsy slur.

I reach towards him and put my hand on his shoulder, not to reap but to try to get a glimpse of what happened.

I see a black phone on a side table in a warmly lit bedroom. Beyond the phone I see Viktor sitting in an armchair watching television, smoking a cigarette and sipping on a dark spirit in a crystal tumbler. My focus returns to the phone as it rings. Viktor stands with the cigarette and tumbler in hand as he walks over to the phone, his eyes staying on the television. He sets down his drink on the polished wooden table and picks up the receiver.

"Da?" Viktor draws on his cigarette.

Viktor exhales smoke through his nose and replies in Russian while looking at his heavy, gold watch. I can't hear the phone call conversation nor do I understand what they're saying.

I see a side door open and a tall young woman with bushy blonde hair and perfectly applied heavy makeup steps into the room and sits on the bed. She crosses her legs and her white satin robe opens to reveal long shapely legs. She watches Viktor as she lights a cigarette. There's something amiss with this young woman, but I can't put my finger on what it is.

"Do skoroy vstrechi." Viktor hangs up the phone then picks up the crystal tumbler and knocks back the rest of his drink in one gulp. He sets down the tumbler and reaches for his back holster, which is resting beside his keys. He feeds the holster through his belt so it sits snuggly at the small of his back. Viktor checks his ammunition in his pistol before he slides it into the holster. He shrugs into his coat and fishes his wallet out of the inner pocket.

"Are you ok to let yourself out?"

"Where are you going?" Her deep and husky voice surprises me. It out of sync with her feminine appearance. In the same way her pink glossy lips belie her strong jawline.

"Dimitri called. He needs to see me at the varehouse. Something about a late shipment." Viktor pulls a small wad of cash from his wallet and places it on the bedside table.

She tucks the money into her purse. "Same time next week?"

"Yeah, thank you Hayden." Viktor straightens his collar as he walks through the door.

My vision is dark and murky. When the gloom clears I see the outline of a neglected warehouse close to the docks. I'm behind him seeing everything he sees. Viktor pulls at a large steel sliding door whose screams announce his arrival. As Viktor enters the building the vision slips away from me. I open my eyes and look down at Viktor who has slumped in the car seat sometime during my vision. I lift my thumb off his body and see a translucent essence clinging to my finger like bubble-gum. He hasn't got much time left. I nudge Viktor awake.

"Think about what happened."

I close my eyes again and concentrate. Viktor walks into the warehouse

"Dimitri, ty yeshche zdes'?" Viktor looks down at his watch.

Thud!

Everything goes black and I feel a tap on the back of my head like I've been hit, but I know it's just an echo of the impact Viktor felt.

Viktor opens his eyes and sees a pair of leather boots and black trousers in front of his eyes. One foot shoves his body onto his back and the assailant straddles Viktor's chest. Viktor's eyes adjust to the bright light behind the assailant's head and makes out a tall helmet with a silver badge on its front.

"Brian..."

Blackness again and I feel a tap on my jaw.

"Vhat da fuck?" Viktor, filled with adrenaline throws his arms up and rolls his body with full force to his side, throwing Brian onto his side. Brian struggles back on top of Viktor and throws another punch which Viktor blocks with his arm.

"For a little fella you throw your weight like one the big boys." Brian goads Viktor in their struggle.

"Vhat you vant, tithead?"

"I want my debts cleared."

"Hah! Not on your life. Vhich is vorth nothing now." Viktor

spits blood into Brian's face.

Brian clutches Viktor's throat with one hand and snatches a handkerchief from his pocket to wipe his face. Brian leans in close and taunts Viktor with a nasty chuckle. "That's where you're wrong, Viktor. Your death is gonna clear my debts."

Brian throws another punch and Viktor tries to jerk Brian off him with some success. Viktor reaches around his back and wrenches his gun from its holster. Brian wrestles with Viktor and the gun slides across the concrete floor.

Viktor looks towards the gun then scampers after it. Viktor clutches at Brian's pant leg and yanks hard. Brian falls to his knees and Viktor clamours toward the pistol. Brian throws himself on top of Viktor and punches him again, Viktor turns his head to lessen the impact on his face. The two men are holding each other by their shirt collars.

"Vhy you do this? Don't ve pay you enough, Pig?"

Viktor throws his body to one side in an attempt to shake off Brian's grip, but Brian reaches for his police-issued baton and strikes Viktor on the head. I feel my head sway slightly and my vision distorts. Brian dashes towards the discarded pistol as Viktor staggers to his feet.

"Dimitri sends his regards, Comrade." Brian pulls back the trigger and a loud bang echoes through the warehouse.

I feel pain where Viktor has been shot and clutch my abdomen to protect myself from this imaginary injury. I open my eyes and see Viktor staring at the car's ceiling muttering words of prayer. Even the biggest and most fearsome men fear death and the afterlife. I close my eyes again to see if there's any more of the vision to be seen.

I'm back in the warehouse. Viktor falls to his knees. The pain is sharp for me, so it must be like getting surgery without anaesthesia for Viktor.

Brian wipes the fingerprints from the gun and tucks it into the back of his belt. Viktor falls on his side and grasps the bloody wound that's spewing dark red blood onto the concrete.

Brian reaches for his radio.

"Bravo Oscar 29. Shot fired near St Katharine's docks. Blue sedan seen leaving the scene. On pursuit of vehicle. Units and paramedics required at the docks. Casualties unknown."

Viktor's voice is croaky and seems to come from a long way away. "I von't die here, O'Malley. I'm coming after you... and Dimitri."

Brian chuckles. "You'll be dead before the paramedics find you." Brian turns on his heel and strides towards the steel door, slamming it behind him.

Everything goes black again.

I open my eyes and look at Viktor. He's ghostly white and his lips have ceased their murmuring. I move my hand away from his body and his essence comes with me.

Viktor's spirit is an older man, perhaps in his fifties. He lurches towards me and throws me to the ground, wrapping his hands around my throat. I'm caught off guard and a little surprised but not afraid as I know he can't kill me.

"You fucking bitch! You could have saved me!"

His hands are tight and I gasp. "I-I couldn't have done anything..."

"I vant revenge and I'll start vith you."

"Please, I'm trying to help."

"I told you to take me to the hospital or I'd kill you, Ava. This is on you!"

I see the bright light of a portal in the corner of my eye.

"Look into the light! You can move on."

"I need to live! Vithout a cat, the mice will run free."

I grab at his hands and try to pry them from my throat. I'm amazed at the strength of this spirit. I'm feeling light-headed and weak.

I look into the light and see a handsome young man leaning out of the portal looking on the scene. He calls out to Viktor. "Moy malen'kiy lev, pochemu ty bespokoish'sya s ney?"

Viktor is focused on me but his attention is broken for a moment and his hands slacken enough for me to drag a lungful of air. I don't know if it'll work but I jerk my knee into his groin. Viktor lets out a guttural groan and his hands shift from my neck to his crotch. I claw at the grass to get out from under his body.

The young man is gesticulating wildly and screaming out in Russian.

Viktor calls out to him but doesn't take his eyes off me. "You know nothing vill get between me and revenge, my love." Viktor speaks in English and I think his words are for my benefit as well as his dead lover.

"Forget about revenge. You can be happy with him." I point towards the portal in the hope that Viktor will turn around and see the light, but his focus remains on me. I wish Niklaus was here, he'd know what to do.

Viktor hauls himself to his feet. His face looks enraged and though I don't think his anger is solely directed at me, I fear I will bear the brunt of it. I clamour into a standing position and prepare for his next attack. He can't kill me but I don't know to what extent he can hurt me. Viktor runs towards me. I side step at the last moment and he tackles thin air and falls onto the grass. I grab the collar of his shirt and with all my strength I lift him into a seated position and force his face towards the light. Viktor's body slackens and his rage dissolves. I let go of either side of his face.

My work is done.

Viktor stands and walks towards the light. The young man in the portal holds out his hand and Viktor takes it, drawing him into an embrace as the light implodes on itself.

I breathe a sigh of relief once the portal disappears. "Fuck my existence." I collapse onto the grass and lay there watching the sky change colour till night has completely descended.

CHAPTER 32

I wander up to the maternity ward and sit on the bench facing the newborns. A small child sitting to my right is swinging his legs back and forth while looking in my direction.

"Hello Ava," the little boy says. I look to my left to see if someone is approaching, but there's nobody there. I look at the small boy and he smiles at me as he continues to swing his legs back and forth. I cock an eyebrow and peer closer at the child.

"My little sister is being born today." The child looks towards the window and all babies. I reach out and poke the small child

"Ouch!" He looks at me scornfully.

"You can see me?"

"Of course."

The child looks healthy and I can't hear the familiar TING in my head.

"How?" I asked dumbfounded.

"It's me. Albert. Well I was. My name is Mackenzie now."

"Albert? You came back?"

"Of course. I made you a promise. I'm sorry it took so long, I had to get older and then I had to get here somehow. I didn't expect to see you for some years yet but then my mum went into labour near this hospital so they brought her here instead of the public hospital."

Albert's face is cheerful, excited. Or should I say Mackenzie? I'm struggling to work this new situation out.

"How can you remember me? You're in a new body."

"Well, I told you I'd try and help you and I did. I went to the other side and started to look for someone in charge. Not as easy as you might think, but I kept searching till I found someone who knew someone else who could help. I explained to them what happened and we came to an arrangement."

I must look like an idiot with my jaw slack and my mouth open. Albert/Mackenzie seems delighted by the astonishment on my face, as if he's a primary school kid who's played a huge prank on a grown up.

Albert looks towards the glass again and then back to me "I know you like to sit here sometimes. I remember you telling me. I was going to go look for you if you didn't appear soon."

"I often thought of you, Albert. I thought you were never going to come back."

"I know." The small boy puts his hand over mine and squeezes it hard enough for me to feel comforted through the veil. "I still get to watch over you, Ava."

"How?"

"It's like having one foot on both sides. It's how I keep my memories about my last life. I dream about you sometimes. Watching over you like you did for me."

"I want to hug you so badly."

"You can, I just can't hug you back. It would look weird me hugging thin air."

I slide myself across the bench and wrap my arms around Albert's small body. I don't have to push through the veil to feel his warm skin, or the fur on his jacket against my cheek. I embrace him for a few moments then kiss his forehead. I feel a tightness in my throat as tears spring from my eyes and flow down my cheek. I feel truly happy for the first time in a very long time. Albert has found a way to release me, a way for me to die. I've waited decades to pass on. Having a hospital to wander through endlessly doesn't take away from the fact that I'm a prisoner.

"I missed you too, Ava, but it's like I never really left you. I was always keeping an eye out for you."

I lean down and clutch his small hand and hold it. "How do I get out of here Albert?"

"You just need to die."

"But I can't die here. I've tried too many times to count, and in various ways."

"I know, but it's different now." A beat. "You don't have to kill yourself right away if you don't want to. I saw you with Niklaus."

"Niklaus."

My goal was always to escape him, but now I'm not so sure. Avaline's memories have weeded their way into my mind and I feel differently about Niklaus.

They haven't changed so much that I wouldn't want to leave this place.

A middle-aged lady strides down the corridor heading for Albert

"Och, there you are Mackenzie. What are you doing out here all on your own? Do you not want to meet your new baby sister?"

Albert jumps up off the bench. "A sister!"

"Aye, and your mother's wanting to see you Laddie, so don't be dallying"

"Ok, Nanna. Can I hold the baby when we see Mummy?" Albert trots after her.

"We'll see. We canna have you dropping the wee bairn."

As the pair are almost out of sight, Albert turns around and waves goodbye to me. I stand and stare at the empty corridor then swing my eyes around to the babies in their cribs. Some are sleeping, one or two crying and one is lying quietly looking around at the strange new world it's found itself in. What must it be thinking of?

I pivot around and stride out of the maternity ward and head for the stairs to the roof.

As I walk up the stairs towards the roof, each step takes me closer to my destination. It could finally be all over and I'm not sure how I feel. While I'm hopeful that I might finally be able to move on, I'm sad to leave Niklaus behind. Avaline has made her home in my head, reminding me occasionally that being with Niklaus isn't just physical. A small part of me has grown attached to him, in spite of my efforts to resist him.

I reach the roof. The sun is peaking over the horizon and its light is conquering the night. I walk towards the edge of the building and climb up onto the ledge. I wonder if this is what Evelyn McHale must have felt like as she stood on the edge of the Empire State Building, but whatever her problems were, I'm sure she didn't endure as long as I have. I've seen the London skyline evolve over decades and today the winter morning sun is glinting off the Thames and I feel a wrench to be leaving it. This is the last time I'll see the world before me. I hope to open my eyes and see a light brighter than the sun and that it will consume me, leading me to an afterlife that has been closed to me for decades. I close my eyes and stretch out my arms.

"What are you doing?"

I could recognise that voice anywhere. I put down my arms and take a step away from the ledge to turn to him.

"Niklaus."

Niklaus is leaning on one leg with his arms crossed over his chest. "You know you can't die here."

"Why are you here Niklaus?"

"I don't know. You felt weird to me. Happy and sad at the same time. I wanted to know what could make you feel that way."

I bite my lip but it doesn't prevent a tear rolling down my cheek. "I can die, Niklaus."

"What?"

"Albert came back and he told me I can die now."

Niklaus straightens up and takes a few steps closer to me.

"Albert? The old man in the coma ward?"

"He's not old now. He's been reborn."

"How do you know?"

"He told me he'd come back for me. And now he has. He said he's got one foot on either side."

"What do you mean? That doesn't happen."

"I just had a conversation with him. He was a small boy who could see me. He remembered my name."

Niklaus looks down at the gravel on the roof, his eyebrows are squeezed together. I'm not sure if he's angry because I'm trying to leave, or whether he's trying to work out a puzzle.

"So what happens now? How does he say you get out?"

"I'm not sure. We got interrupted. But he said I can die now." The pain in his eyes is too much and I turn back to the London skyline and hear my boots scrape back towards the ledge.

"No don't."

I turn back towards him. "This is what I want Niklaus. I need to die."

"Come on Ava, let's talk about this.

"No Niklaus. This is the way it was always meant to be, I was supposed to die during the war." I indicate to the world around me and say, "I was never meant to be here. I don't think we were ever destined to reconnect."

"Ava, listen to me... look at me." His voice is stained and his arms are flailing as he tries to shift my attention away from the skyline. "I love you. I don't want you to leave me."

His words and their intensity draw my eyes towards him. "I know."

Niklaus looks distressed as he tugs at the roots of his hair.

"Don't you love me Ava? Not even a little? Because the way we've been together recently says different."

I turn from him and open myself to the bone-chilling dawn and run a hand through my long hair. A single strand falls away from my locks. I let it go and watch it be carried off by the wind. I need a moment to consider my feelings before I answer him.

"The truth is, I do. I do love you, Niklaus."

Niklaus freezes and I can see in his eyes that his heart has skipped a beat.

"...but it's not enough." I fling my arms wide and take a step back as I push my heel off the ledge. I hear Niklaus screaming my name as he races to the edge of the building. Halfway down I close my eyes and all I can see is darkness.

CHAPTER 33

E verything hurts.

I open my eyes and there's no bright light.

My body is splayed across the footpath outside the hospital. I draw a breath and inhale dirt and dust. I cough and reflexively take a deeper breath that sets of a convulsion of coughing. I see the glaring light of early morning. The last few stars of the night sky are fading. I haul myself up into a sitting position, each movement sending shockwaves of pain through my body that resonates with the thumping in my head. I lean my head into my hands.

I look around expecting to see Niklaus, but there's nothing and nobody – just a deserted car park. I reach out to the low brick wall of a garden bed and use it to steady myself as I stand on wobbly legs. I'm overwhelmed with sudden nausea. I take a moment to recognise this feeling but it's too late – my body instinctively lurches forward and throws up bile into the garden. Ironically I think perhaps it's not so great to be human after all. Then I laugh, loudly

"I'm alive!"

I smile so widely my face hurts. I close my eyes and take a moment to enjoy every ache I'm feeling. The chill of the morning air caresses my cheeks and I smell a sweet perfume. Jasmine! I look around and see the perfect white flowers cascading over the brick wall. I lean over and sniff the petals, enjoying the sickly floral scent, mixed with a sour acidity, then look down and see the bile I just ejected. I laugh again at the wonder of the unfiltered world. The colours are brighter and the lines of the trees and buildings are clean and crisp. I look down at my clothes and the tank top that was black before is now green and my jeans are blue denim. My boots and trench coat are still black, but maybe they already were in the beginning. It was so long ago I can't remember their original colour, nor whether I stole them or Niklaus found them for me. My attention shifts from my exterior to the internal and I realise my mouth is parched and I'm surprised to find I'm ravenous. I haven't felt hungry in decades.

I wander into the hospital and head straight for the kitchen. I look through the window in the door and see the staff preparing breakfast for the hospital's patients. I move towards the double swing doors with the intention of walking through them but my body pushes them with a loud squeak. I quickly retreat, remembering I'm no longer invisible. I leave the kitchen area and head to one of the closest wards. Every ward has a pantry that stores basic food for patients between meals. I slip in and grab a can of lemonade and a sandwich from the fridge and take it to a waiting room close by. The taste of fresh bread with ham and cheese explodes in my mouth and brain. I sit back on the lounge chair and sip my lemonade after scoffing down my first meal in decades.

Now that my primary needs have been met I find myself thinking about Reeves, Matthews and even Nicole. I probably won't be seeing them again for a long time. Then I think of Margie. I've watched her age over the decades, followed her life and subsisted on her highs and lows and right now she's at a low point. I watched her try to kill Bardon to provide vigilante justice when the system failed; and saw her disappointment when she couldn't do it. Even with all the strength I know she has, she couldn't bring herself to kill someone when her life has been dedicated to saving people.

I stand and swallow the last of my fizzy drink. I wander into the empty corridor and slip into the clean utilities room. I find a 20ml syringe, a blunt drawing up needle and two ampoules of sterile water and slide them into my pocket. The ward is semi-dark and my black trench coat helps me blend into the shadows. I know where I'm going, but I keep slipping into patients' rooms to avoid nurses who are making their morning rounds.

I reach Bardon's door without being seen, twist the door handle and slip into the room. Bardon's window blinds are open and the dawn brings helpful shadows that guide me towards his bed. Bardon is asleep, looking like somebody's grandfather. Soft snores reverberate between his slightly open lips and as I lean over I see his overgrown nose hairs vibrating in rhythm with the snores. He looks older than the last time I saw him when Margie collected his blood while he was on trial. I can't help wondering how he can sleep so peacefully after all the horror he has inflicted on others.

I withdraw the syringe from my pocket and draw up 20mls of air. Barden is hooked up to fluids, I feel around for the IV port and attach the syringe. I slowly inject the line with air, then I disconnect the syringe and draw up another 20mls of air and push it into his IV line. I feel around in my pocket for the blunt needle and water. I attach the needle to the syringe and draw up all the liquid and I push it through the port. That should hide the air I've just administered, once it pushes through the line and into his body.

It's funny how I haven't forgotten my medical training, even though I haven't practised since the war. I still remember the ward sister chastising me for leaving bubbles in a syringe before administering medication to a patient. A 20ml dose of air is likely to cause disruption in Bardon's system – 40mls will ensure his demise. Especially since he's an old man with a heart condition.

I leave his room and stroll back down the corridor towards the exit doors that I've longed to walk through for many years. I can just hear the faint echo of Bardon's heart monitor shrieking as I leave the ward. Nurses push past me with apologies as they rush towards the emergency buzzer.

I walk out into the brisk morning and succumb to the pleasure of crisp air in my lungs and the crunch of gravel under my boots. I turn up my coat collar as I leave the hospital grounds. I don't know where I'll go or what I'll do – everyone I used to know thinks I'm dead. Maybe I'll find a way to retrain as a nurse, pick up where I left off.

Whatever happens I intend to make the most of this second chance at life – being Death's captive has left me with no fear of the afterlife.

KEEPING CALM

AND

CARRYING ON

Scarlett Reed

A flurry of people move about the hospital. A new batch of wounded allied soldiers were brought in overnight, and the number of causalities has exceeded the hospital's capacity. Men who can stand are clustered in groups, smoking cigarettes with shaky hands while they wait to be seen by overworked doctors and nurses. The corridors are lined with stretchers for those who can't mobilise and the groans of injured men echo down the once barren halls. British intelligence has relayed that the Luftwaffe have planned an attack on London tonight, so I've organised some medical students from my department to take fire-watching shifts on the roof when the raid begins. Looking at my watch I notice that shift change must have already occurred, so I might be able to catch Ava before she goes back to the nurses' quarters. I delve into the deep pockets of my white coat and pull out a packet of Chesterfields and my lighter. I flick the lighter open and emblazon the wick. Leaning into the flame an ember forms and I breathe deep to inhale the smoke.

I turn the lighter over between my fingertips. It was my father's during the Great War, and then he gave it to my brother when he enlisted as a good luck talisman. My father had it engraved for him – 'ER' in cursive letters. Edward Reeves, another causality in the war against Adolf. Nobody expected it to last this long, and nobody seems to know when it'll end. Flipping over the lighter I look at the crude scratching on the polished silver that my brother added, it reads 'live today to die tomorrow'.

As I walk through the double doors into the general ward I scan the blue uniformed women and spot her leaning over a soldier with a gunshot wound, filling in his details onto a sheet of paper on a clipboard. I loiter around nearby beds, picking up charts and glancing blindly at them while staying within earshot, but it sounds like Ava will be a while yet. I pluck a pen from my pocket and tap the chart in my hand.

"Excuse me Nurse, could I have a word with you for a moment?"

Ava gives me a startled look then lowers her eyes. "Oh. Yes, Doctor, of course."

I guide her towards the doorway and lean in closer, pointing my pen at the chart as I speak. "I need to see you after your shift."

"Elwood, I can't. You're married. I can't do this anymore."

"I know. I thought about what you said and you're right. I think I have a solution, a compromise…"

"Doctor Reeves!" Dr Dancovitch's voice booms across the room and all eyes are on us for a moment. "Are you going to commandeer Nurse Adams's attention? Or can she continue with her patient assessments?"

Ava blushes and scurries back to the waiting soldier. I return the chart to the end of the bed, snatch up a freshly rolled bandage and move to a soldier with a head wound. The ward falls silent and movement ceases momentarily as the air raid siren blares. It won't be long before the Germans are bombing us overhead. As I triage patients my eyes keep being drawn to Ava. Occasionally our eyes meet, making me think, or maybe hope, she's also watching me work.

An explosion close to the hospital radiates a shudder through the ward. Everyone stops and gasps, worried faces looking at each other for reassurance. Out of the sudden silence a shrill scream and we all turn our heads to the sound. A patient has woken shrieking as he claws at the bedsheets, trying to remove them. Soldiers either side of him hold him back.

"We have to get to the trenches!" the patient screams while fighting off the two men.

The two officers try to settle the man back into bed. I hear whispered words of reassurance. The patient isn't cognitive to time or place so he continues to throw himself out of bed to take cover, grabbing at the soldiers holsters for a weapon to defend himself.

I grimace as I reach for a vial of tranquilizer and a syringe. As I'm drawing up the dose of medication a gunshot echoes through the room. I turn towards a groan of pain. I watch as a wardsman grasps his thigh and falls to the ground. Dr Dancovitch rushes over to him and applies pressure over the bloody wound.

"Esther, get gauze and bandage!" Dancovitch's niece drops the linen she was holding and runs out of the room. "Reeves!"

I turn towards Dr Dancovitch's voice. His face is contorted into a deep snarl.

"Don't just bloody stand there! Put him down for Christsake!"

The patient is screaming, waving a gun in the air out of the officers' grasp.

I turn my attention back to the medication in my hand. I draw up double my intended dose and pull the needle out of the vial.

BANG!

Another shot. I run over to the patient who is struggling against both men. I plunge the needle through his clothing into his thigh. The patient's screams lose their intensity and within a few moments his body slackens. I scan the room. Nurse Margie and a wardsman are rushing toward a nurses who's lying on the floor. I frantically look around the room for Ava. My heart lurches and my breath catches in my throat. I throw the syringe on the bedside table and race to her. I fall to my knees, pushing others out of the way so that I can turn her over onto her back.

"Ava!"

I shake her. No response. I look her over for damage. A small blood stained wound to the abdomen. I put my hand on the wound and look up at a nurse. Without saying a word she nods and runs off in the same direction as Esther. I feel her wrist for a pulse.

I can't feel anything.

My heart is pounding and my mouth is dry. The nurse returns with gauze. I move my hand away so she can apply pressure to the area. My shaking hand moves to her throat to seek her carotid artery. My fingertips desperately probe for a pulse. Perhaps it's the adrenaline pumping through my system, but I can't feel anything. I lean forward and put my cheek close to her face. I can only stand this proximity for mere seconds.

"Dr Dancovitch!"

My mind is swarming with possibilities and I can't focus.

A trolley arrives, I pull Ava's body up into my lap. I hold her for a moment then wrap my arms under her legs and lift her up onto the trolley. Dr Levi Dancovitch approaches with a stressed but controlled expression. He touches her neck. Margie pulls a compact mirror from her apron pocket and holds it out. Dr Dancovitch holds the mirror under Ava's mouth and nose. The reflective glass doesn't fog. My heart is in my throat and the world feels as though it's crashing down around me. I take several deep breaths to push down the rising sense of loss and grief, but that's an impossible task so I stumble towards the exit instead.

The corridor is filled with soldiers so I trudge past them in a daze, blindly seeking a place of privacy. As I reach the men's lavatories a sob escapes my lips. I feel relief momentarily but my body is no longer my own. Tears flood my eyes, welling over and running down my cheeks. It was an abdominal shot – how can she be dead? Was it the shock?

No. Even if she died from shock she would have lingered longer. What could I have done?

I wrack my brain for every life-saving intervention I could have provided. My brain is spiralling out of control.

If I had drawn up the tranquillizer faster, would she have lived?

I put my head in my hands and weep uncontrollably. My brain is being cruel to me. Asking me questions like – what could I have done differently? How could I let this happen? It was an abdominal shot, not fatal. Not fatal. How could she have died so fast?

"Dr Reeves?"

My ears register a female voice. I hadn't heard the door open. I lift my head and see Ava's best friend, Margie, standing before me.

I wipe my face on the sleeve of my lab coat. I try to look composed, but Margie's expression of sadness and concern reflects my failure. We're standing a few feet from each other in a silent impasse. The knot in my throat is growing so large I'm struggling to swallow.

Margie approaches and places a hand on my shoulder. Her makeup is smudged and her cheeks are wet with tears. It is my undoing. I bring my hand to my face to cover my eyes as fresh tears spew forth. Margie presses her body against mine and wraps her arms around my waist.

My sadness evaporates momentarily. My first thought is how unprofessional this must look. A nurse hugging a doctor in the men's bathroom. If anyone walks in there would be a scandal. I'm about to push her away when I hear a sob. Hearing a woman crying affects me at a primal level. I wrap my arms around her and focus on comforting Margie. The burden of Ava's death doesn't feel as heavy knowing that I'm not alone in my grief.

"There was nothing you could do."

Hearing her say that makes me almost believe it's true.

"She died so fast. I don't understand..."

Margie tightens her grip around me and sobs again. "Nor do I."

She releases me and takes a step back then looks at her uniform. Her white apron is covered with blood – transferred from my clothing. I look in the mirror and notice a smear of blood on my cheek. Ava's blood.

"You should get changed." Margie is untying the bow of her apron.

I look down. My coat, shirt and pants are splashed with dark red. Margie bundles up the soiled apron.

"I need to get back to the ward, Elwood." She turns and walks towards the door.

I turn to the basin and run the tap to wash the blood off my hands and face. I hear the door click shut behind her.

I pull out a fresh set of clothes from my locker and throw my soiled clothing in the bin – there's no point bothering to clean clothes I couldn't bear to wear again. My reflection shows bloodshot eyes and I look weary beyond my years. I'm only twenty-eight but a middle-aged man stares back at me with grief etched into his features and auburn stubble on his chin.

I push Ava's death to the back of my mind and shift my focus to the injured soldiers lining the hospital corridors. Whenever my mind drifts back to her lifeless face I chastise myself silently. Compartmentalise, Reeves.

I walk back to the ward. Ava's body has been removed. Dancovitch's niece, Esther – who shares his dark hair and slim features, is on her knees wiping up a pool of dark blood off the floor. I had seen so much blood as a doctor and the sight of it never fazed me, but knowing it is Ava's makes me queasy and the memory of her death floods back to me like a tsunami wave. I turn my back on the scene, I can't stay here with the incident still bombarding my mind. I glance down at my watch and see my shift is already over. I remember that the only reason I was staying back was because I wanted to speak to Ava. The image of her lifeless body hits me with such force that if I don't move forward I will most certainly fall back.

* * * * *

I want a whisky, but the barman says they're out so I settle for a pint of ale. Damn rationing. The image of Ava's lifeless body keeps flashing before my eyes. The only thought that gives me solace is that there was nothing I could have done. I still can't understand how she died so fast. I've seen many soldiers with multiple gunshot wounds who have lasted longer. Did I want that though? For her to linger, confused and in pain? Of course not, but there would have been a chance that I might have saved her. Or at least said my final goodbyes to her.

I loosen my jaw and allow the amber liquid to slide down my throat in one long effortless swallow. I motion for the barman.

"Are you sure you want another?" A look of concern crosses his face.

"I'm not causing any trouble, and my day has been long and hard."

The barman hesitates for a moment then pulls me another pint.

"You should slow down before you fall down," he says then he turns towards a group of uniformed soldiers who are flagging him down.

I pull a cigarette from my packet and ignite it with a flick of my brother's lighter. 'Live today to die tomorrow'. Edward's inscription is particularly apt tonight.

I feel a gloved hand on my shoulder and a feminine presence beside me at the bar.

"I feel like a drink after today too."

Margie motions to the bartender. She climbs onto the wooden barstool beside me. "How are you feeling?"

I draw on my cigarette. "It keeps replaying in my head. It happened so fast, it's all a blur."

Margie nods

The barman approaches Margie.

"Gin and tonic, if you have it."

"Yes madam."

"Put it on my room," I interject as Margie reaches for her purse.

The barman nods, serves her a drink then moves away.

"You've got a room?"

"I can't go home tonight. My wife is trying to fix our relationship. I can't handle that while I'm processing Ava's death."

"The ward sister has given me the day off tomorrow. To grieve."

I look at Margie's composed features.

"You seem to be handling it pretty well."

The alcohol seems to be affecting me more than I anticipated. My words spill out almost as I'm thinking them.

For a moment I think she hasn't heard me as she continues to caress her glass and looks deep in thought.

"I don't think I've realised she's dead. I just feel numb." Margie delves into her purse and pulls out a cigarette. I pick my Zippo off the bar and hold it to her cigarette. Margie leans into the flame and puffs lightly.

"I have to pack up her belongings tomorrow and take them to her mother in the East End."

We sit in silence for a few minutes then drain our glasses and order another round. During this silence my mind comes back to why I wanted to speak to Ava. I wanted to tell her I'm going to leave my wife after the war.

"I don't think I can go back to the nurses' quarters tonight. Last time I was there she was alive and well. All of her belongings are there just where she left them."

I can understand why she doesn't want to go back. If I was surrounded by her belongings I would go mad with grief.

"I have a suite upstairs. You can have the bed and I'll take the couch."

I know it's improper to offer such an arrangement to a single woman but I want to help. My words have once again bypassed my reason and shot straight to my mouth.

"Thank you. But I'll take the couch."

I had expected her to say no. I look at her naked ring finger and consider how it would look to others if she came up to my room with me. I put my hands under the bar and slide off my gold wedding band. I place it on the bar and slide it discreetly toward Margie.

Margie gives a tight lipped grimace. I don't think she had considered the social implications of my offer. She picks up the ring and puts it on her wedding finger.

"Thank you."

I give her a curt nod then motion to the barman for another round of drinks.

My legs feel a little wobbly as Margie and I walk up the stairs towards my suite. My decision for another round before the bar closed wasn't the greatest. I hold open the door for Margie to walk through and I notice her gait is also affected. Margie collapses onto the couch and I sit next to her. I cross my feet on top of the adjacent coffee table. She lights two cigarettes and hands one to me. We're all talked out after hours in the bar, reassessing our relationship that was only defined by our mutual association with Ava. Now there's just the silence of grief and comfort.

Margie removes my wedding band and glides it onto on my left ring finger.

"What about in the morning when you leave?"

Margie chuckles. "I'll keep my hands in my pocket."

I clasp her hand and give it a squeeze. "You've been a welcome distraction this evening. I feel better for having you here with me." I release her hand. "You're a lot like her in some ways."

Margie stubs out her cigarette and turns to face me. "How so?"

I stub out my cigarette in the ashtray and turn towards her. "You're easy to talk to. You have the same sense of humour." I look at Margie's face and that's where the similarities stop. Margie has a heart-shaped face with soft angelic features. Her full lips beckon me, promising to remove all the pain and sadness I currently feel. I touch her face and rub my thumb over the border of her lips. She doesn't flinch away from my touch. I lean in and kiss her. Margie returns my kiss and pulls me closer to her.

* * * * *

Movement in the room wakens me. Margie, dressed only in

her undergarments, is moving around the room collecting her clothing. I sit up in bed and she turns to me.

"How's your head?"

I am surprised by her question. The atmosphere in the room is heavy.

"It's been better. Nothing a little aspirin won't cure."

Margie slips into her dress, and sits on the edge of the bed to fasten her shoes.

"Did you know your wife once accused me of sleeping with you? She said I looked the type. I guess she was right."

My eyebrows peak. "My wife?"

"Yeah, she confronted Ava and me outside the hospital. She shook me up while shouting accusations. Ava told her the truth to stop her assaulting me."

My mind reels. "How did I not know this?"

"You and Ava broke up soon after. We assumed you knew."

I sit there dumbfounded. How could my wife not tell me? I consider confronting her, before realising I don't care enough about the relationship to try and repair it.

Margie turns to face me. "I appreciate you letting me stay here last night but we can never do this again."

"I feel like I should say sorry."

"That's guilt Elwood. I feel it too. We did the wrong thing by Ava."

"We came together because of her."

"We shouldn't have taken things as far as we did."

"So, what do we do now?"

"We go back to our prescribed relationship and we don't mention this again."

Margie bows her head and her hand reaches up to wipe her cheek.

I think it has finally hit her. Ava isn't coming back and Margie can't confess she has done wrong by her. And nor can I.

Margie collects her coat and leaves the hotel suite without looking back.

* * * * *

I've read over this patient's chart for what seems like the fifth time. I can't concentrate. I keep thinking about Ava. Conjuring more complex and detailed fantasies about us reuniting or reliving memories and moments with her. I would have cherished her more if I knew my time with her was so short.

"Reeves!"

I snap back into reality. Dr Dancovitch towers over me. While his features rest naturally with a look of displeasure, in this instance it seems purposeful. He shoves a chart into my hands.

"This is the third medication error you've made this week, Reeves. Where's your head been for the past few weeks?"

I open the chart and read through the medications.

"Oh."

I had written one ounce instead of one fluidram for a strong opioid medication. The dosage would have killed the patient.

"Oh indeed! It's fortunate my niece was caring for this patient and she brought it to my attention."

I should feel bad, or at least offended, that a subordinate is disrespecting the hierarchy. Instead I feel numb and apathetic. I've been going through the motions of my professional duties while my head is reliving the past.

I am on my final round before I hand over to the next shift. The pep pills I took earlier in the shift to help me concentrate on the task at hand and get out of my own head are losing their effectiveness. I need to get home and sleep, but I can feel eyes watching me. I look up to see Margie approaching me, the fabric of her nurses' uniform enhancing her blue eyes.

"Dr Reeves?"

She gestures for me to move away from the patient's bedside. I put the chart at the end of the bed and move with her into the centre of the ward.

Margie leans in close and whispers. "I need to see you after your shift."

My eyebrows peak with surprise. Margie's last words to me on that morning several weeks ago still ring in my head. *We can never do this again.*

Perhaps she has reconsidered. This moment isn't ideal. I feel fatigued, but if I reject her now I may never get another opportunity.

"I'm finishing up now. I can meet you at the hotel bar in an hour."

She nods. My colleague walks onto the ward and gives me an expectant look. I excuse myself and go to hand over my patient notes to him.

* * * * *

Clean shaven and smelling fresh I wait at the bar for Margie, swirling the rare treat of a Scotch whisky around the base of my tumbler. A foreboding sense of guilt washes over me – I know Ava would disapprove of my affair with Margie. I shouldn't be here but it's hard to resist Margie's company when it alleviates some of the grief I feel.

The hum of soldiers' voices dips for a moment and in unison all heads turn towards the doorway. Margie spots me and glides through the crowd, ignoring their appreciative gazes. I wave to the bartender and I order Margie a gin and tonic. It arrives as she approaches the bar.

Margie glances at the stool beside me then surveys the room. "Can we sit in a booth?"

I nod and pick up both drinks as we make our way towards a vacant booth. Margie's expression is sombre, perhaps she's feeling as guilty as I am, but I'm certain she'll loosen up after a few drinks. We slide in close together. Margie reaches for my packet of Chesterfields that I've placed on the table. I look at her hands and notice a gold band on her wedding finger – that encourages me to rest my hand on her thigh and lean in to kiss her.

"I'm pregnant."

I stop before my lips reach hers – frozen momentarily as I process her words. I pull back and my hand jerks away from her thigh. Her words rattle around my mind. My hand reaches for my Chesterfields and I light a cigarette. I take a deep breath and watch the smoke spew forth and add to the hazy gloom of the bar.

"Did you hear me?"

"I heard." I flick the ash into the tray. My words tumble out uncensored. "You can't have it."

"Obviously." In the moment it takes Margie to light a cigarette, a wave of relief washes over me. "That's why I'm here. I need your help."

"What do you need? Money?"

Margie's face goes bright red and she hisses into my ear.

"No. I need you to get rid of it."

This is not how I expected my night to progress and I struggle to arrange my thoughts.

"I'm not that kind of doctor."

"But you must know doctors who can..."

"Ask around the nurse's quarters. Some of them must have been in a similar situation."

Margie's chest heaves and she wipes her cheek.

My compassion overrides my panic as I hear her sob. I lean back into the chair and wrap my arm around her shoulder. She leans into me while playing with the gold band on her finger. Margie's emotions settle and she regains her composure. I remove my arm and we sit in silence smoking cigarettes and sipping our drinks.

If I can't be the one to do it for her I should at least pay for it to be done. I delve into my jacket pocket and retrieve my wallet. I'm glad I went to the bank after my shift, in anticipation of enjoying a night out with Margie. I withdraw a five pound note and rest my hand with the money on her thigh under the table.

"I don't know whether it's enough, but it's all I have on me. Let me know if you need more."

* * * * *

I haven't seen Margie for several days. Ordinarily I would be unconcerned. Sometimes our shifts don't coincide, but I have a niggling feeling something is wrong. I dismissed these feelings for the first two days. It's day three now, so I discreetly check the nurses' roster. My tension eases as I see Margie has had two days off and is due on shift this evening. I'm tending to a young woman who received burns to her legs when a bomb went off and splattered her legs with factory chemicals. As I cleanse the wounds and remove grime, my eyes dart back and forth to the door. Finally shift change is apparent when nurses burst into the ward and swap notes with the nurses about to leave.

I can't see Margie.

I'm familiar with most of the faces and some of the names, but don't feel confident to ask any of them about Margie, except maybe Esther Dancovitch. She's a quiet girl who keeps to herself and isn't likely to gossip. I continue washing my patient's wounds while watching Esther and waiting for an opportunity. Esther collects medical equipment to be sterilised and takes them to the dirty utility room. I gather the bloody gauze and dirty bandages together in a heap, excuse myself from my patient and follow after Esther.

Nurse Dancovitch is sorting through dirty equipment. I dump the bloody gauze into the bin and the bandages into the linen basket. I need to sound casual.

"I haven't seen Nurse Conner for a while. I thought she was supposed to be on shift tonight?"

I hear a clatter of equipment fall to the floor. I turn my head to Esther.

"She's been unwell for the past few days, Sir."

"Nothing serious, I hope?" It's a strain now to keep my tone light.

Esther collects the items from the floor and reorganises them. She's shifting her weight from foot to foot and opens her mouth a couple of times to speak, but bites her lip instead.

I wait. I want answers.

"She has a fever and some abdominal pain. My uncle thinks it's the flu."

"Dr Dancovitch?"

"Yes. I was worried when she wouldn't come down to dinner. Marg– er... Nurse Connor wouldn't let me send for help, so I asked my uncle to come and review her."

Shit. Dancovitch isn't an idiot. He'd know it isn't the flu.

"Is she still in the nurses' quarters?"

"No, my uncle took her to the Royal. He was worried the staff would be too distracted if she was here."

"And he is absolutely correct. Perhaps I'll send flowers. Nurse Connors should know we're thinking of her. Let me know if you hear any news."

"Yes, sir."

Esther's face is unreadable and I can't keep up this charade any longer. I give her a nod and turn back to the ward.

* * * * *

Last time I was in this bar, Margie was sitting beside me. Now I'm alone, apart from the uniformed soldiers who appear never to leave. I look into my pint glass, straight through the dregs of amber liquid to the wooden bar. I could have done more. I could have asked around maternity for a doctor who was willing to help her. If I had done some research I'm sure I could have found some medication or herbs that could bring on a miscarriage, but instead I gave her money and hoped for the best. Ava must be looking down on me with fury for not taking care of her friend.

"Hello." The voice comes out of nowhere. I turn to see Margie standing before me, neatly dressed in a black dress and a fur lined coat.

"Margie!" I gesture to the empty seat beside me. Margie seats herself and reaches for my packet of Chesterfields. I delve into my pocket for my lighter and hold the flame steady as she draws her first puff.

"I heard you were sick. I was planning to visit you at the hospital."

"Probably best you didn't."

"What happened? Are you still...?"

"No."

"Did the police make enquires?"

"No." She drew on her cigarette. "We're in the clear. Maybe they've got more pressing matters to attend with a war on. Dr Dancovitch referred me to a colleague of his, an old friend who he said would be discreet."

I inwardly chuckle to myself. "His friend will think it was his."

"He's married." Margie looks almost offended.

"So am I."

"You don't act like it."

"I'm unhappily married. Is it wrong to look for comfort in the arms of another?"

"It is when it's your mistress's best friend."

The accusation stings. I don't have to explain myself, but maybe I'm trying to work it out for myself.

"I never thought of her as my mistress. Our relationship was more than physical. She was my sweetheart. I was planning to leave my wife after the war ended."

Margie shakes her head. "They always say they're going to leave their wives. Most never do."

"Well it doesn't really matter now, does it?"

"No." Margie exhales a breath of smoke and flicks ash into a nearby tray.

"I'm sorry, Margie. For everything." It seems inadequate, but I can think of nothing else to say.

"What do we do now?" Margie's face is composed and hard to read.

I sit and consider for a moment. My heart still feels heavy with the burden of Ava's death, and though Margie is a comfort, being with her fills me with guilt. "We go back to being colleagues, maybe friends. We keep patching up soldiers until this hell is over."

No flicker of emotion crosses her face. She stubs out her cigarette and picks up her purse and walks through the smoky haze, past the rowdy soldiers and out into the street.

Scarlett Reed is an Australian author and nurse who has a wandering imagination and several unfinished works. After creating a bucket list in which finishing a book was at the top of the list she choose one of her a story ideas and gave herself one year to complete a rough draft. Six months and one day later Death's Captive was written. Scarlett Reed is a pseudonym.